(#5)

JUNIOR HIGH

THE EIGHTH GRADE TO THE RESCUE

JUNIOR HIGH

#5

JUNIOR HIGH

THE EIGHTH GRADE TO THE RESCUE

Kate Kenyon

SCHOLASTIC INC.
New York Toronto London Auckland Sydney

ISBN 0-590-40899-2

12 11 10 9 8 7 6 5 4 3 2 1   7 8 9/8 0 1 2/9

Printed in the U.S.A.   01

First Scholastic printing, July 1987

Chapter 1

"Something's up," Nora Ryan said, as she and her best friend, Jennifer Mann, approached Cedar Groves Junior High.

Their eighth-grade friends stood on the front steps as always, waiting for the first bell. Below them Jason Anthony, in his camouflage fatigues, tic-tacked his skateboard across the walk.

"Looks like business as usual to me," Jennifer said.

"Nobody's talking," Nora pointed out.

She was right. Usually bubbling over with news in the morning, their crowd stood quietly watching someone or something coming up the walk toward the school. Everyone was so absorbed, they didn't notice Jennifer and Nora coming up the stairs toward them.

"What's happening?" Jennifer asked.

"Denise and *Tony*," Tracy Douglas said

with a dreamy look in her blue eyes.

Jennifer followed Tracy's gaze. Just out of earshot, Denise Hendrix, her blonde hair gleaming in the morning sun, stood facing her black-haired brother, Tony.

Nora laughed. "The way you say 'Tony,' Tracy, you'd think we'd never seen him before."

"I haven't seen him in months," Tracy said.

No one — not even Denise — had seen much of Tony since he started going with Jessica Hartnett. Denise had complained about the change in Tony more than once. A week or so ago, she had announced, "Jessica and Tony have broken up. Finally, things'll get back to normal." Now, judging from her gestures, there seemed to be more trouble between her and her brother.

"Are they arguing?" Jennifer asked in disbelief.

Though two years apart, Denise and Tony shared an unusually close relationship. Heirs to the Denise Cosmetics fortune, they had depended on each other through one family relocation after another. Before coming to Cedar Groves in September, they had gone to school in Switzerland.

Lucy Armanson ran her hand through her curly black Afro. "Can you imagine fighting with *him*?"

"Isn't he a hunk!" Tracy Douglas said.

Jason Anthony's freckled face popped up in front of them. "I didn't know you cared," he said, making an extravagant bow.

Ignoring him, Susan Hillard said, "Oh, Tracy, you think anything in pants is a 'hunk.'"

"This time she's right," Jason said. Striking a classic body-builder's pose, he turned his head to the right and made a muscle with his arm.

Tommy Ryder came up behind him laughing. "Give it up, Anthony. It's me they're talking about."

"What are you doing on the outside?" Jason asked him.

Usually, Tommy came to school through the indoor walkway that connected the high school to the junior high. If the high school girls, amazed to see an eighth-grader in their territory, peered at him, he figured his magnetic good looks had turned their heads. It made his day.

Jason gave Tommy a good-natured punch in the arm.

Tommy said, "Who do you think you're punching?" and punched Jason back.

The girls sidestepped them both for a better view.

"He's okay," Mia Stevens said about Tony, "but he's not a very sharp dresser."

Jennifer and Nora exchanged amused glances. Mia was into punk. Today, her spiked hair was striped orange and purple to match her outsized orange sweater, a purple tank top was visible on one shoulder, and paisley leggings were tucked into her black combat boots.

"It wouldn't take much," Mia continued. "A leather collar'd do wonders for him." Her boyfriend, Andy Warwick, had a whole collection of dog collars, one for every day of the week and a pink rhinestone one for special occasions.

"I think he looks real sharp," Tracy said.

"Between *his* alligators and polo ponies and yours," Susan Hillard said sarcastically, "you two could open a preppy zoo."

Jennifer was about to defend Tracy when Mitch Pauley ambled over tossing a baseball in the air. "What's everybody looking at?"

"Tony Baloney," Jason said. He bent over and picked up his skateboard. "They're demented. They've got this thing about older men. A classic search-for-a-father syndrome."

The boys nodded their heads in agreement.

The girls laughed. Tony Hendrix was only sixteen years old!

"Jason's right," Mitch Pauley argued. "Remember old Cliffie."

Earlier in the year, Cliff Rochester had replaced their English teacher, Mrs. Rickerts, when she left to have a baby. The boys had not forgotten what they referred to as "The Class Crush." Neither had the girls. They still found Mr. Rochester attractive. Now, however, they thought of him as a good teacher rather than as an object of their affections.

The bell rang. In a flurry of activity, everyone gathered belongings and rushed through the school's double doors. Jennifer hung back. She didn't like to see anyone argue, but it was especially distressing to see Denise and Tony cross with each other. She had tried to pattern her own relationship with her younger brother, Eric, on the Hendrixes'. Like Denise and Tony, they, too, had special circumstances that made their closeness important to her: Their mother had died when they were very young. Of course, Eric was too young to share any real confidences with, but she hoped that would change in a year or two.

Tony had hold of Denise's arm. If he didn't let go, she'd be late.

"Denise!" Jennifer called to her friend. "Hurry up!"

Denise broke loose and came running up the stairs. Jennifer held the door for her. As Denise breezed through it, Jennifer looked back. Tony hadn't moved. He looked incredibly lost.

The whole thing is so sad, Denise thought on her way to her locker. Here was her happy-go-lucky, self-assured big brother acting like a wimp all because of a girl like Jessica Hartnett! Even the name made her angry. She hadn't liked Jessica from the beginning. She was patronizing, treating Denise as though she were a five-year-old, introducing her as "Tony's baby sister."

Denise yanked open her locker door. The small mirror inside reflected a tight, anxious face. Jessica Hartnett would never look like that, she thought.

Tony believed Jessica was perfect. Too perfect, thought Denise. Plastic perfect. Jessica always smelled of hair spray. And those long fingernails! Grotesque. She carried polish with her for repairs, and she had dropped out of computer class when she broke two nails on the same day. Even then, Tony hadn't wised up.

That was the worst of it: Tony. It broke her up to watch him suffer so; at the same time, she was disappointed in him for having fallen for someone like Jessica in the first place. In Switzerland, Denise had liked all of Tony's friends. She had bragged about his good taste in people to her new friends in Cedar Grove — until Jessica.

Jason Anthony careened down the hall on his skateboard. When he saw Mr. Donovan, the principal, rounding the corner at the end of the corridor, he hopped off, tipping the board front up with his foot so that he could grab it.

"Quick!" he said, shoving the board toward Denise. "He's coming this way! Stash this in your locker."

Looking directly at Jason, Denise slammed her locker door shut and turned on her heel.

Jason didn't have time to protest. Holding the skateboard behind his back, he swung around. "'Morning, Mr. Donovan," he said, smiling braodly.

"Good morning, Jason," Mr. Donovan said, adding, "Get rid of that skateboard," as he marched past.

Jennifer caught up with Denise. "Are you okay?" she asked.

Denise shrugged and slowed her pace.

Even with the pinched look on her heart-shaped face, Denise was beautiful. Her skin was flawless and her delicate coloring was heightened by whatever strong emotions she was feeling.

"Anything I can do?" Jennifer asked her.

Denise smiled at her friend. Sweet, sensitive Jennifer. Why couldn't Tony have picked someone like her? Jennifer would never hurt anyone the way Jessica had hurt Tony. "There's nothing anybody can do," she said.

Jennifer stopped so abruptly that a couple of grumbling students plowed into her. She didn't seem to notice. She shifted her books to one hip and said, "There's always *something*!" and planted her free hand on the other hip.

Denise laughed. Standing there in the middle of the hall with boys and girls streaming past her, tall, thin Jennifer was like a rock in a river. Not a bad comparison. Jennifer was strong and unyielding in the face of trouble. She devoted herself to helping others. There were her causes: Save the Whales, Feed the World. And she wasn't just talk; she was always writing letters, volunteering at the animal shelter, visiting the old and the sick. The T-shirt she wore under her open oversized shirt said it all: SO MUCH TO DO . . . SO LITTLE TIME.

"Maybe something can be done," Denise conceded, "but I don't know what."

"What you have to do," Jennifer said, "is define the problem. Once you do that—"

"Define the problem," Denise echoed, wondering where to begin.

Nora rushed up beside them. Breathless, she said, "The problem is that you two have lost it. Homeroom's back there about half a mile."

Denise sighed. "We'll never make it."

"Oh, yes, we will!" Nora said.

With compact, determined Nora in the lead, they dashed into Room 332 just as the sound of the second bell echoed down the hall.

At lunch period, Steve Crowley stopped Jennifer and Nora as he was leaving the cafeteria and they were entering.

"Would you two be on my committee for the hayride?" he asked.

The hayride party at the stables and adjacent forest preserve outside town was a late fall tradition. Steve, whose father was in the restaurant business, had volunteered to chair the food committee.

"The party's not for weeks," Jennifer said, thinking of all the things she had to do between now and then.

"Only two," Steve reminded her. "We got a late start because of the Washington trip."

"When's the first meeting?" Nora asked.

Steve smiled. He knew he could count on them, and they on him. The three of them had been friends since kindergarten. "I'll let you know," he said.

"Nora! Jen!" Tracy Douglas called as she hurried toward them. "I've been looking all over for — " When she saw Steve, she stopped cold. He was so tall and handsome. And so self-assured! Not at all like most of the boys in their class. She'd been trying to get him to notice her since seventh grade. Maybe today was the day. "Hi, Steve," she said, smiling her most devastating smile.

Steve's blue eyes twinkled. "Hey, Trace," he said. "You'd better hurry or there won't be any meat loaf left."

"Meat loaf!" the girls exclaimed in horrified unison.

Meat loaf had never been one of their favorite dishes. Since the eighth-graders had been allowed to run the school for a day earlier in the year, and Mia Stevens had been the 'Meat Loaf Maker', even the word made them cringe.

Steve laughed. "It's not so bad if you close your eyes and hold your nose."

Jennifer and Nora raced through the thinning cafeteria line, bypassing the meat loaf, and hurried to their special table in the center of the room. Tracy stopped to pull an extra chair over from a nearby table.

"Hey, Tracy," Tommy Ryder called from the next table, "We've got an empty place; why don't you sit here?"

Jason Anthony hooted. "Even if she did, it'd still be empty!"

Tracy stood there looking confused.

Susan Hillard tugged Tracy's sweater. "Sit down!" she ordered disgustedly.

Tracy sat. "Wasn't that nice of Tommy?" she said. "And Jason's so funny."

The others groaned.

Nora dug into her salad. "I bet they put sulfites on this stuff," she said.

"What are sulfites?" Lucy Armanson asked.

"Sulfites are chemicals sprayed on salad ingredients to keep them fresh and crisp-looking," Nora began. Since she planned to be a doctor, Nora was interested in nutrition. At the slightest opportunity, she could easily make a lecture out of the subject.

Susan pushed back her chair. "Lucy, when're you going to learn not to ask Nora questions like that?" She took up her tray and stalked off.

Ignoring her, Nora went on, "They can cause serious allergic reactions."

They all focused on Nora's salad: Wilted, washed-out green lettuce mixed with light orange tomato wedges streaked with green, plus an array of indistinguishable, colorless ingredients.

"You don't have a thing to worry about," Mia said.

Denise slipped into a chair. She was wearing dark glasses. From behind her came the sound of chairs scraping on the worn linoleum floor.

"Spies," Amy Williams warned.

Denise glanced over her shoulder. The boys had knotted together at the end of the table to eavesdrop. She pulled her chair in and leaned toward the girls. "Have you seen Tony?"

No one had.

Denise pushed the sunglasses to the top of her head. "What a relief! He said he wanted to see me at lunch."

"What's going on with you two?" Jennifer asked.

"He's driving me crazy. That's what. *Jessica Hartnett, Jessica Hartnett*. That's all I hear!"

"Didn't they break up?" Tracy asked.

Denise nodded. "Jessica did. Tony refuses to accept it. He follows me around talking about her, asking for advice."

"What he needs is some exercise," Amy Williams said. She wanted to be a gym teacher and thought physical activity was the cure for all ills. "He used to be real active but lately — "

"A sympathetic ear is all he needs," Jennifer offered.

"Right," Nora said. "It takes time to ... heal."

"It's been two weeks," Denise complained. "If he doesn't get over it pretty soon, I won't have an ear left."

Jason leaned further back in his chair.

"Speaking of ears," Nora said loud enough for the boys to hear, "some people we know have awfully big ones."

Tipping his chair back, Jason said, "All the better to hear you with, my — " The chair slipped. Jason lost his balance and fell backward, landing at Denise's feet. " — dear."

"Oh, no," Denise said. "There he is!"

Tony stood at the other end of the room looking around.

Jason smiled up at her. "I've always been here, Denise," he said. "You've just been too cruel to notice."

Denise slipped the dark glasses over her eyes and slid down in her chair. "Tell him I'm not here."

Too late. Tony had spotted them.

Denise moaned as he came toward them.

Tony was only steps from the table when the bell rang.

Chapter 2

Sitting cross-legged in the center of Nora's bed, Jennifer said, "It's not like Denise to be so mean."

"It can get pretty annoying," Nora said. "Sally nearly drove me crazy last year when she broke up with her boyfriend."

Jennifer was surprised. Nora's sister Sally was a university freshman and a dancer. She had always seemed so independent. "You never said anything."

Hugging the calico cat pillow Jennifer had made for her birthday, Nora fell back across her bed. "You were away or something."

"Last year?" Jennifer searched her mental calendar. "The only time we went away was over Thanksgiving."

"That's when it was," Nora said.

"I was only gone four days."

"Believe me it was long enough. Sally

used up a year's worth of emotion in that time."

"If I were really in love," Jennifer said, "and it didn't work out, I don't think I'd get over it that fast."

"A person can't sit around feeling sorry for herself," Nora said. "Life goes on."

"That's easy to say," Jennifer countered, "but what if — " She broke off. It was difficult to imagine herself or Nora in a similar situation. Neither of them had been in love. She herself had never had a real date. "Well, how about Brad Hartley?"

Brad Hartley was in Nora's shop class. After the eighth grade trip to Washington D.C. a few weeks ago, he had taken Nora out for pizza and a movie.

"Yeah," Nora said, hugging the pillow closer, "how about Brad Hartley!"

Jennifer giggled. "You know what I mean. What if he . . . called the whole thing off?"

Nora sat up. "What 'whole thing'? We had one date, Jen. That's not exactly a major romance."

"But he really likes you," Jennifer said.

"You think so?"

"I know so."

"How can you tell?"

"The way he hangs around you in shop for one thing."

"That's because I'm good at it."

"It is not."

Nora laughed uneasily. Sometimes, even with Jen, conversations like this made her uncomfortable. She thought of herself as a serious person, and she wasn't always sure that her interest in boys and clothes was in keeping with that image. "What're you saying? That I'm not good at shop?" She tossed the pillow at her friend.

Jennifer kept it. "You know what I'm saying, Nora Ryan. Face it: You are a very attractive person."

Nora made a face. "I'm too short and my hair's too curly."

"You're not short; you're petite. Boys like that. Look at that Jessica Hartnett. I'll bet she's not even five feet tall. And Tony's at least six feet!"

"Maybe that's why she broke up with him: She got tired of standing on her toes to hear him."

"You can laugh," Jennifer said. "But if you were as tall as I am — "

" — I could sit in a deep chair with my feet touching the floor," Nora said wistfully, "and reach high shelves and wear fantastic clothes and — "

" — Your patients would *have* to look up to you," Jennifer teased.

"No problem," Nora said. "I'll be a pediatrician."

"Just make sure your patients aren't older than ten."

They both laughed. Then, growing serious, Jennifer asked, "Do you remember when we were the same size?"

"A century ago," Nora said.

"Fourth grade." Jennifer traced the cat's outline with her index finger. "That was a really good year. Remember how we were always partners in line?"

"Partners in everything!"

"Sometimes, I wish we were back there."

"You're not serious."

Jennifer nodded. "I don't mean *always*. Just sometimes, you know?"

"Why?"

Jennifer shrugged. "I don't know. We were such good friends."

"We still are. Better!"

That was true. Still, things had changed. Then, there were just the two of them. Nothing else seemed to exist. Now, Jennifer had her causes, and Nora, her determination to be a doctor. There were boys and clothes and electives, and all kinds of choices to be made.

"Listen, Jen," Nora said trying to fathom her friend's mood, "if you're worried about Brad Hartley — don't be. No *boy* could ever come between us."

Brad Hartley was not the issue. No boy was. She and Jennifer would always be friends. She didn't doubt that. It was just that the world had become a bigger place. An exciting, unpredictable place. But often a scary place. She stood up. "Who? Moi? Worry?" she said. Then she threw the pillow at Nora and ran out of the room.

By the time Jennifer had done her homework, washed her hair, and settled down to phone Nora, her serious mood had passed.

"What're you wearing tomorrow?" she asked, as one or the other asked every evening.

"I don't know," Nora answered. "The weather's so changeable."

"The weatherman said it might be unseasonably warm."

"Then it'll probably rain," Nora said.

"If it's nice, maybe we could stop at Temptations after school."

"Can't. I've got a dentist appointment. Only good thing is I've got an early dismissal."

"So, what're you going to wear?"

"I don't know. How about you?"

"The slacks and shirt my father brought home last trip." Jennifer's father seemed to like shopping for her — especially when he was away on a business trip. Usually, the clothes he chose were too babyish, but this outfit was sensational. It was a soft emerald green rayon set with a long-tailed blouse that could be worn in or out. "If I don't wear it soon, it'll be too cold and I'll have to wait till spring."

"If it still fits," Nora said, adding, "You know what'd look great with it?"

"Your scarf — the long one with all the colors," Jennifer said.

Nora laughed. "Sometimes I think we share the same brain."

"Keep the brain," Jennifer said. "Just bring the scarf to school tomorrow."

Next morning, Nora arrived at school before Jennifer. When she saw her friend coming up the walk, she ran down the front stairs waving the scarf like a flag.

At the bottom of the steps, Jason Anthony grabbed it out of her hand.

"Give that back!" Nora called after him as he sped off on his skateboard.

He was looking over his shoulder at Nora and didn't see Jennifer in front of him.

"Jason!" she shouted as she stepped onto the grass. "You're going to hit somebody!"

He turned and hopped off the board, which came racing toward her. She jumped to avoid it and dropped her books.

"You — ! You — !" she sputtered.

"Terminal creep?" Jason offered as he waved the scarf in her face.

She reached out to grab it. Too late.

Tommy Ryder ran up alongside her and snatched it. He balled it and passed it off to Mitch Pauley, who ran with it.

Nora blocked his way. "Give me that scarf!"

Mitch gave her a wide-eyed innocent look. "Sorry, Nora," he said. "I didn't know it was yours."

"Give it to me!" she commanded.

He held it out to her. When she reached for it, he moved it to one side. She reached again. He stretched it out high over his head. She should have known he'd do that. As captain of the football team, named the best all-around athlete, Mitch made a contest out of everything.

Nora stood her ground. "I am not going to play this game, Mitch Pauley. You just give me that scarf."

Jason whizzed past, grabbed the scarf, and disappeared around the side of the building.

Mitch smiled smugly.

"He is a real jerk," Nora said as she helped Jennifer pick up her books.

"Which one?" Jennifer asked.

"All of them!" Nora answered.

"Jason'll give it back," Jennifer assured her. "What would he do with a girl's scarf?"

Just then, Tracy Douglas came around the corner of the building, wearing the scarf around her neck, the ends flying out behind her.

Jennifer and Nora looked at one another. Answering Jennifer's question, they said, "Give it to Tracy!" in unison.

They caught up with Tracy as she went through the double doors into the hall.

"Tracy, that's my scarf," Nora said.

Tracy put her hand to it as though she thought Nora would snatch it from her neck. "Jason gave it to me."

"But he took it from me." Nora was impatient. Sometimes Tracy drove her crazy.

Jennifer said, "It really is Nora's, Tracy. She brought it for me. We thought it'd look good with this outfit."

Tracy surveyed Jennifer from top to bottom. Then she took off the scarf and held it against Jennifer's shirt. "I don't think so," she said. "Too distracting."

The three of them went into the girls' room to check it out. Jennifer tried tying the scarf several different ways. Nora made small adjustments. In the end, they decided Tracy was right. She wasn't very discriminating about boys — she liked them all — but she had good clothes sense.

"You look just perfect plain," Tracy said.

Jennifer laughed. "Thanks a lot."

Tracy blushed. "Oh, I didn't mean — "

Tracy might be a bit spacey, but she didn't have a mean bone in her body. Jennifer liked her for that.

"I know what you mean, Tracy," Jennifer assured her. And she did. The outfit looked smashing with only the gold chain she wore around her neck and the small gold balls in her ears. It didn't need anything else. It was a no-frills outfit on a no-frills girl.

"You know what you could do?" Tracy asked. Then, without waiting for an answer, she unbuttoned the bottom button of Jennifer's shirt. "Tie the ends like this."

Jennifer stood back from the mirrors over the sinks to get a better look. "Thanks, Trace," she said. "I like that."

The bell rang before Nora had the chance to fold the scarf and put it in her bag. As she hurried toward homeroom, the scarf draped over one shoulder, Jason sneaked up behind her and slipped it off. Before she knew it was gone, the scarf was floating down the hall ahead of her.

Nora chased Jason into homeroom. He was standing on Mr. Mario's chair tying the scarf to the top of the flag pole in the corner.

She marched over to him. "Give me that scarf, you creep!" She took hold of the chair.

Behind her, a voice said, "There are

rules about flag display, Mr. Anthony."
Mr. Mario!

Jason smiled sheepishly. "Yes, sir," he
said. "Someone . . . tied this scarf here. I
was . . . uh . . . just . . . getting it down.
Nora asked me to."

"Is that right, Nora?"

The room was quiet. Nora heard the
clock whir as it did when the bell was about
to ring. There was no time for a long ex-
planation. If she simply said yes, it might
look as though she'd put it there; if she
said no, Mr. Mario might think she was
trying to keep Jason from taking it down.

She sighed.

The bell rang. "We'll get to the bottom
of this later," the teacher said wearily.
"Give me the scarf, Jason."

Jason handed it down to him. Mr. Mario
folded it neatly and put it in his top desk
drawer. Jason jumped off the chair and
went to his seat.

Looking up from his desk, the teacher
asked, "Aren't you forgetting something,
Jason?"

Jason looked perplexed. "I don't think
so."

"My chair."

"I don't have it," Jason said.

Mr. Mario took a deep, audible breath.
"Neither do I," he said.

Jason skipped to the front of the room

over the feet thrust into the aisle to trip him, did a deep knee bend, lifted the chair, whirled with it, and took three giant steps to return it to Mr. Mario's desk.

Everybody clapped. Jason bowed.

Sometime during the morning, the wind shifted out of the south sending springlike air seeping under the doors and through the windows of Cedar Groves Junior High. By lunchtime, the scarf was forgotten. So were books and studies — everything but the moment.

In the bright beams of sunlight streaming through the dirty windows, the cafeteria's pea-soup green walls and worn linoleum looked even dingier than usual. The girls ate quickly and went outside.

Sitting in the wooden bleachers beside the athletic field, Jennifer stretched her arms out wide as if to embrace the world. "Isn't this incredible! We should do something special today. Ride bikes, fly kites. Something!"

"Try 'go to the dentist,'" Nora said as she bit into an apple.

"How could I forget that?" Jennifer said.

"Easy. You're not the one going."

Everyone was busy after school. Denise had Drama Club; Amy, softball practice;

Tracy and Lucy, shopping; Mia, a date with Andy.

Jennifer was the only one with nowhere special to be, nothing special to do. Since she was usually the one rushing off to meetings, it was a welcome change. She took her time at her locker, checking her assignment notebook, gathering the right books, listening to the sounds of slamming locker doors and shouting voices echoing down the hall. She closed her own locker door quietly and smoothed the Save the Whales banner on it with her hand.

Outside, she closed her eyes and took several deep breaths. She envisioned green buds on the bushes fronting the school and high in the trees along the walk. In her mind's eye, even the grass was lush and green. She opened her eyes to a thinning, dry lawn with brownish patches and trees whose last leaves had lost their color. It didn't matter. Under the clear sky and the golden sun in her new green outfit, Jennifer felt at one with nature.

A sudden burst of energy propelled her down the stairs two at a time. At the bottom, she began to run.

Behind her a voice called, "Jen? Hey, Jen!"

She turned.

Tony Hendrix jogged up beside her.

Chapter 3

"Have you seen Denise?" Tony asked Jennifer.

"Drama Club meeting," Jennifer told him.

He looked crushed. "Oh, yeah. I forgot."

"That's because you aren't the one going," Jennifer said, repeating Nora's line to her about the dentist.

Tony looked puzzled.

Jennifer thought she'd explain; then decided against it. But there Tony was looking at her with his sad dark eyes as though he were waiting for her to say something.

"Nora had to go to the dentist," she began, "and I forgot about it and when I said, 'How could I forget?', Nora said — " Tony looked more confused. "Forget it," she said. "It wasn't all *that* funny."

"You probably had to be there," Tony said.

"Right," Jennifer said.

Then nobody said anything.

Finally, Jennifer said, "If I see Denise, I'll tell her you're looking for her." She edged away.

"I'll probably see her before you do," Tony said.

"Oh, yeah. Right. Then you can tell her I *wasn't* looking for her."

Tony laughed. "I'll do that." He looked at her long and hard with narrow eyes.

It made Jennifer uncomfortable. She shifted her books to one arm.

"Where're you headed?" Tony asked.

"Home. It's such a beautiful day, I thought I'd walk."

Tony glanced around as though he hadn't noticed the day at all. It gave Jennifer a chance to really look at him. With his dark eyes and olive skin, he was extraordinarily handsome. But he seemed uncharacteristically ragged around the edges. Unusually long, his black hair curled over his shirt collar; there was a spot on his Izod cardigan; one Reebok lace was broken. It made her sad to think that some girl could do this to him.

"It is, isn't it?" he said.

Now, Jennifer was confused.

"The day," he explained. "It is beautiful."

"Like spring," she said, because she didn't know what else to say.

"I guess." He smiled, a sad smile with a frown on it. "Mind if I tag along?"

She felt as though she'd come in in the middle of a movie and hadn't the slightest idea what was happening. She twisted a lock of hair with her index finger. "Where?"

"Didn't you say you were walking home?"

"Oh, yeah. Home. Right."

"Do you have the feeling we should begin this all over again?"

She laughed. "I'm not sure it'd help."

They fell into step alongside one another.

"I like to walk," he said, "but after Monday I don't suppose I'll be doing much of it."

Was he going to sprout wings? she wondered. Or evaporate into the green-gold springlike air? "What's Monday?"

"I take my driver's test. I was pretty excited about it for a while — up until. . . ." His voice trailed off.

"It *is* exciting," she said. "You'll have a driver's license and everything."

"If I pass."

"Oh, you'll pass," she said enthusiastically. "You're good. I've seen you in the Driver's Ed car and — " She broke off. He'd think she'd been watching him.

"If I pass, I pass," he said. "If I don't — " He shrugged.

They lapsed into silence. Jennifer searched her brain for something to talk about. Talking to Boys was a subject she and Nora often discussed. They thought it was a good idea to ask the boy about something that interested him. Tony was interested in Jessica Hartnett. Jennifer certainly couldn't ask him about *her*.

Suddenly, she heard herself blurt, "Are you okay?"

It took him so long to answer, she thought he hadn't heard. But when he said, "How do you mean?" she knew there was no way to take back the words. She just had to plunge ahead.

"Well, I don't know exactly. You just seem different. Kind of pale and . . . thinner."

He nodded. "I haven't been taking such good care of myself, I guess."

"Oh, you should. It's really important. If Nora were here, you know Nora Ryan, she's going to be a doctor, she'd tell you how important it is to eat right and get exercise and stuff. Preventive medicine, she calls it."

He chuckled. "Too late for that."

"It's never too late," Jennifer said.

They were at the corner. As they waited for the light to change, Jennifer could feel Tony looking at her.

"Has Denise said anything?" he asked.

"About what?" She knew full well what he meant. It made her feel dishonest to pretend not to. But she couldn't very well say, "Denise told us all about you and Jessica — that she threw you over and that you're driving Denise crazy over it."

"Me," he said.

The light changed.

Jennifer stepped from the curb. "She talks about you all the time. She really thinks you're . . . special."

"About me and Jessica," he clarified.

"Only that you, ah, broke up."

He was silent for several seconds. Then, he said, "It doesn't matter."

Did he mean it didn't matter that Denise had told her, or it didn't matter that he and Jessica had broken up? She didn't ask.

Finally, he said, "Do you know her?"

"Jessica Hartnett?" Jennifer asked. "I know who she is."

"What do you think of her?"

She didn't have an opinion about Jessica. She knew what Denise thought of her, but Jennifer tried not to make judgments based on other people's opinions.

"She's very pretty," she said.

Tony smiled. "Beautiful! But it's not just her looks. There's . . . something about her." He seemed suddenly energized. "When I first met her," he continued, "I was kinda put off. She seemed reserved.

Maybe aloof is a better word."

Denise would have said stuck-up, Jennifer thought. It was curious how people could see the same quality in someone and call it by a different name.

"But after I got to know her — "

The words continued to pour out. It was as though Tony had been all bottled up and someone had removed the cork. Jennifer was happy to walk along beside him, listening. She was flattered that he trusted her enough to open his heart. She hoped someone would feel about her someday the way Tony felt about Jessica. Jessica couldn't know how much he cared. If she did, she certainly couldn't have broken off the relationship.

Somewhere in the periphery of her mind, Jennifer heard a car horn. She looked around.

Although Tony didn't seem to hear the horn, he was sensitive to Jennifer's reaction. "Listen, Jen, I'm sorry," he said.

"For what?"

"This is all so boring."

"I don't think it's boring," she put in quickly.

He laughed. "I'm even boring myself!"

They were at Tony's street. Jennifer hesitated, ready to say good-bye, but Tony kept walking.

"Your street," she said.

"I'm in no hurry. If you don't mind, I'll walk you home."

Mind? If the best-looking, nicest boy in the whole sophomore class walked her home? "It's okay with me," she said coolly, though her heart raced.

At her door, he smiled. This time there was no frown following it.

"Denise says she's lucky to have you for a friend," he said. "Now, I understand what she means."

Jennifer could feel herself redden. Not knowing what to say, she said, "Thanks."

He laughed. "That's my line," he said. "Thanks for listening. You are really easy to talk to."

Jennifer was surprised to find that it was after four. She felt as though she had just left school and, at the same time, been away from it for hours. Confusing — as though her walk with Tony had slipped out of its time frame to stand apart.

Jeff Crawford, the Mann's male housekeeper, found her staring at the clock. "Don't tell me that's not working," he said. "That's all I need. The coffeepot erupted this morning, the vacuum cleaner died in the middle of the living room floor — " He broke off as Jennifer turned to look at him, grinning.

"Something must have happened," Jeff said, his blue eyes twinkling. "You look enchanted."

"Enchanting?" she said, purposely mistaking his meaning.

"That, too. That's a very becoming outfit. Your father's taste seems to be improving."

"My father's taste is wonderful," she said. "He's wonderful! You're wonderful! Everything's wonderful!" She opened the cookie jar and extracted two freshly baked chocolate cookies.

"Those aren't," Jeff said. "They're burnt."

Jennifer took a bite. "You're right; they're not wonderful."

"I warned you."

"They're . . . superb!" She took two more cookies and headed upstairs, leaving Jeff openmouthed behind her.

In her room, she closed the door and leaned against it, looking around as though she were seeing this place for the first time. It was a lovely room. Banners of golden sunlight streamed in the windows, and passed through the crystal whale on her desk to break into shimmering rainbows. Her chenille bedspread gleamed newly washed white. She walked toward the long mirror over her dresser, looking at her reflection as though it were an approaching stranger.

"Hello," she said to this new person. "How are you today?"

"Wonderful!" said her reflection.

"You certainly look wonderful," Jennifer said to her tall, slim green-clad self. The color of her new outfit brought out the green in her hazel eyes.

"You look older," she said, as her reflection did a model's turn. "At least" — she leaned in for a closer look — "fifteen."

Satisfied that she couldn't have looked better if she had planned to meet Tony today, she went to her desk and opened her math book. But her gaze kept drifting to the window, and her mind kept replaying her conversation with Tony.

Once they got over the initial awkward moments, she had been comfortable with him. He said she was easy to talk to. Actually, he had done most of the talking. Maybe that was the key: being a good listener. Of course, it might be different if they'd had a real date. Still, they had been alone. She'd never been alone with a boy before except to do an assignment or to talk to Steve Crowley. But she couldn't count him. They'd grown up together. He was more like a brother than a *boy*.

She sighed. It was all so confusing. She

opened her top desk drawer and took out her diary. Ms. Gunter, their seventh-grade English teacher, had encouraged her students to keep a journal. Running her hand over the blue leather binding, Jennifer thought she probably would have kept a diary anyway. Putting her thoughts on paper helped her to sort them out; sometimes it helped her know what they were.

She sat very still for a long time, her pen poised ready to write. Nothing came. It was if there were too many words coming too fast to catch a firm hold; or there were no words at all to describe what she was feeling.

Finally, she wrote:

Today, Tony Hendrix walked me home.

She sat back. What would Tony say about their time together? Probably nothing. Most likely, he had walked away and forgotten all about it. He was probably home now thinking about Jessica. It was silly of her to get all starry-eyed. His walking her home did not equal his liking her. After all, lots of girls liked him, girls his own age. But he did talk to her, really pour out his heart. Was it only because she happened to be there?

A cloud passed in front of the sun and doused the rainbows.

She left the diary open — she'd come back to it later — and went to call Nora.

Chapter 4

Tracy stopped at Nora's locker. "You won't believe who I saw after school yesterday. . . . Together," she added meaningfully.

Nora didn't respond. She was in no mood for gossip. She had waited outside school for Jennifer until the last minute. Now, if she didn't hurry, she'd be late for homeroom.

"Jennifer and guess who," Tracy persisted.

"I don't have time for games, Tracy," Nora said.

"That's okay," Tracy said. "You'd never guess anyway. Jennifer and — you ready for this? — Tony Hendrix!"

Nora looked at her sharply. "Sure," she said.

"It's true," Tracy said. "My mother was

driving me over to Lucy's, we were going shopping, and — "

It couldn't be true. Nora had talked to Jennifer on the phone twice the day before: once before dinner, once after. Jennifer would have told her.

She closed her locker and started toward Room 332.

Tracy fell into step beside her. " — We honked and everything. They were so involved with each other they didn't even notice!"

Nora turned to go into her homeroom.

"And she's not even here this morning!" Tracy said before she moved on.

Nora slipped into her seat.

"Have you seen Jen?" she asked Jason.

He hadn't.

Denise smiled and waved from the back of the room.

She'd know if Tony was with Jennifer yesterday. There wasn't time to ask her now. Maybe she could catch her before first period. In the meantime, she just wouldn't think about it.

Mr. Mario said something Nora didn't hear. There was a shuffling as everyone got out their notebooks. Automatically, Nora opened hers. Then, Mr. Mario began writing on the board.

He could've been writing a foreign language for all Nora knew. She kept looking at the clock and the door. Where could Jen be? She was never this late. Could she be sick? Maybe she had fallen yesterday, and Tony came along and found her. That could explain why she hadn't mentioned it; if she had a concussion she might have been delirious or something and not even remembered. Come to think of it, she had sounded strange on the phone. Sort of preoccupied. Nora envisioned her friend at home this minute. Unconscious!

She rose slightly in her seat so that she could see out the window. She caught a glimpse of someone running up the walk.

The second bell rang.

"Miss Ryan?" Mr. Mario was talking to her.

Thinking he was calling roll, Nora said, "Here!"

"Part of you anyway," the teacher said.

Everyone laughed.

Jennifer was late. She had forgotten to set her alarm. That, coupled with a sleep that was late in coming and uneasy, made it nearly impossible for her to get herself together this morning.

The second bell rang as she dashed through the school doors and down the corridor, her hair flying.

"Jennifer Mann!" Mrs. Peters called from the office door.

She turned and said, "'Morning, Mrs. Peters," without breaking pace.

"The corridor is no place to practice track," the woman said.

Jennifer slowed to a fast walk. All she needed was detention.

Mr. Mario was writing on the blackboard when Jennifer entered Room 332. She slipped down the aisle to the back of the room.

Without turning, Mr. Mario said, "Good morning, Jennifer. I hope you slept well."

She knew he didn't expect an answer; it was just his way of letting her know she was not going to sneak in unnoticed. But she didn't yet have her mind in gear, as Jeff Crawford would say, and she blurted, "Actually, I had a rotten night's sleep."

Keeping the chalk to the board, Mr. Mario turned his head slowly. "That makes two of us."

Everyone laughed.

Jennifer wanted to sink through the floor. One consolation: Mr. Mario did not send her back to the office for an admit slip.

Across the aisle, Nora was trying to get her attention. When Jennifer looked her way and smiled, Nora mouthed, "I have to talk to you."

Jennifer didn't understand.

Nora tried again. Behind her, Jason

mimicked her, exaggerating her lip movements.

"Mr. Anthony," Mr. Mario said. "Are you in pain?"

Jason's expression froze, his lips thrust out in an exaggerated pucker. "No, sir," he said. "Just, ah, limbering up. Getting my mouth ready for the day." He pulled his lips back into a jack-o-lantern grin, then puckered them again.

"I suggest you exercise your mind first," Mr. Mario said.

This time, there were a few isolated snickers, but Mr. Mario's tone stifled any outright laughter.

When the bell rang, Nora turned in her desk. "Why didn't you tell me about Tony?" she asked Jennifer.

Jennifer felt herself redden. She shrugged and busied herself with her books. She had meant to tell Nora when she called her before dinner, but the vague sense that talking about it then would have made it too real, too ordinary, had stopped her. "Tony?" she said.

"Tracy said she saw you two together."

Jennifer got out of her seat. "I have to stop at my locker. I was so late I didn't have time. I'll tell you about it later."

"I'll go with you," Nora said, but Marc Johnson got between them.

"Got a minute?" he said to Nora.

A transfer student from California, Marc was tanned and tall and good-looking. Nora had had a crush on him when he first arrived, but she had quickly gotten over it.

Jennifer didn't wait to hear Nora's answer. She raced out of the room and down the hall, relief flooding her.

But not for long.

"Hey, Jen," Lucy Armanson called from across the hall. "What were you doing with Tony Hendrix yesterday?"

Several people turned to gape at Jennifer. Nothing like announcing it to the whole class!

Fortunately, Lucy was swept up with the tide and Jennifer didn't have to answer.

This time.

She was climbing into her navy blue gym shorts when Susan Hillard got to her.

"What's this I hear about you and Tony Hendrix?" Susan made it sound like an accusation.

"I don't know, Susan," Jennifer said between clenched teeth. "What did you hear?"

Nora and Denise burst into the locker room, chattering at once. They backed Jennifer into a corner.

"What happened between you and Tony yesterday?" Denise asked.

"Nothing happened," Jennifer said. "It was a nice day and —"

In the gym, Mrs. Scott blew her whistle.

Jennifer sidestepped along the wall. "We'd better get out there." She dodged past several other girls.

Nora, Denise, and Susan rushed after her, firing questions.

"I'll tell you later," Jennifer said as she took her place in line.

Reluctantly, Nora and Denise were about to do the same when Mrs. Scott blew the whistle again. "Hendrix! Ryan! You're not ready for prime time!"

The girls stopped short. They'd forgotten to change into gym clothes.

By lunch, even the boys knew about her and Tony.

Jennifer had no sooner sat down at the table than Jason pulled his chair closer and sat in it backwards, his arms folded across the back. "So," he said, "now it's Tony Baloney," sounding like a weary parent.

"Buzz off," Susan Hillard said.

"I'm only trying to save Jennifer from herself," Jason said.

"Yeah," Tommy Ryder put in. "If she wants a good-looking boyfriend, she couldn't do better than right here in her own class."

"What would she want with you creeps?" Mia asked.

Tommy rose slowly to his full height. "Who're you calling a creep?"

"Look, you guys," Nora said. "Jennifer doesn't need advice from any of you, so get lost."

Jennifer couldn't stand it another second. "This is ridiculous!" she erupted. "You'd think I was dead or a piece of furniture or something the way you're talking about me. I'm sitting right here! And I don't need advice! I don't need anything! You're making a mountain out of nothing! Tony and I just happened to be going the same direction. Period! End of report!" She paused to take a breath. "Now just leave me alone!"

Everyone stared at her silently for several seconds. Then Jason got up and turned his chair around.

"Just trying to help," he said as though he were deeply offended.

The girls busied themselves with their lunches. They were anxious to hear the real story, but they knew better than to push Jennifer for details now.

Nora opened her banana yogurt.

"That looks disgusting," Susan Hillard said.

"It's very good for the digestive system, and the potassium in the bananas makes it especially healthful." Nora said. An automatic response. Her mind was not on bananas and yogurt but on Jennifer, whom she watched as she ate. Finally, she said, "I thought maybe you fell or something yesterday and Tony found you."

Jennifer couldn't believe her ears. "What?"

"I thought maybe you — "

"I heard you, Nora," Jennifer broke in. "Why would you think that?"

"I talked to you twice last night. You never mentioned Tony. So I figured maybe you had amnesia, temporary, I mean, and forgot."

Jennifer sighed. "There was nothing to forget."

"Then why didn't you tell her?" Lucy asked.

"Because there was nothing to tell!"

"That makes sense," Susan said. Why a person did something was far more important, she thought, than what they did. And for the life of her, she couldn't figure out why a man of the world like Tony Hendrix would be interested in Jennifer Mann. "Tony didn't *plan* this or anything."

"He was looking for Denise!" Jennifer said.

Tracy dashed up to the table. Breathless, she said, "Am I glad you're still here, Jen. I thought I'd miss you." She sank into a chair, took a few breaths, then leaned in confidentially. "Do they know?" She cocked her head to indicate the other girls at the table.

"Know what, Trace?" Jennifer asked.

"About you and Tony."

Jennifer groaned.

"The whole school knows," Lucy said.

"That's impossible," Tracy said. "I didn't tell anybody."

"You told me," Nora said.

"Well, you and Lucy. Nobody else." Tracy felt cheated. It was no fun having a secret to tell when everyone already knew it. "If I thought you'd go around telling everybody!"

"There's nothing to tell," Susan said. "Tony came looking for Denise, and Jennifer just happened to be there so he walked her home. No big deal. It could've been any one of us."

Jennifer felt suddenly flushed. The fact that she had come to the same conclusion didn't make it easier to hear.

"If it was me," Tracy said, "it'd be a big deal."

"Only because you'd make it one," Susan said.

Tracy looked hurt until she saw Denise entering the cafeteria. "There's Denise," she said. "Now we'll find out what really happened."

"Someone's walked off with my lunch," Denise said as she sat down. "I've looked all over for it."

"How can you think of eating at a time like this?" Tracy asked.

"Easy," Denise answered. "It's lunch-time."

"Some things are more important than food," Tracy said.

"Like what?"

Everyone but Jennifer said, "Jennifer and Tony!"

"First I heard of it was this morning when Nora told me," Denise said.

"You didn't say he didn't tell you," Nora said.

"I was too surprised," Denise said.

"He didn't mention it at all?" Lucy asked.

"He must have said something," Tracy said.

"Like 'Oh, by the way, I saw your little friend Jennifer this afternoon,'?" Susan said.

Denise shook her head. "Not a word."

Simultaneously, all heads swiveled to look at Jennifer.

Jennifer shifted in her chair. "What have I been telling you?" she said. "It was nothing."

Doing a quick reassessment, Susan

asked, "Then why didn't he tell Denise?"

"For the same reason I didn't tell Nora," Jennifer said. "People don't tell other people everything. Just this morning, Marc Johnson was talking to Nora. Has she said a thing about it?"

Everyone looked at Nora.

"There's nothing to tell," Nora said.

Jennifer looked smugly from one to the other. "See?"

"It's not the same at all, Jen," Lucy said. "I mean, Marc Johnson?"

"If one person doesn't tell, that's one thing," Tracy said. "But when two people don't tell, that's another."

They all focused on Jennifer.

She stood up. "This whole thing is ridiculous! I'm going somewhere where people haven't lost their — " Her jaw dropped. Tony Hendrix was coming toward them. Her heart pounded and her legs felt like used rubberbands. She sank into her chair.

One by one, the other girls followed her stunned gaze.

Tony waved a brown bag toward Denise. "Hungry?" he said to his sister.

"No wonder I couldn't find my lunch," Denise said.

"Sorry. I took yours and mine." His eyes made a casual sweep of the table, stopping when they connected with Jennifer's. "Hi, Jen," he said, smiling warmly.

Chapter 5

"There was a phone call for you," Jeff Crawford said when Jennifer arrived home.

She felt an instant rush of excitement. "Who was it?"

"Steve Crowley. Something about a committee."

"Oh." Hoping Jeff didn't hear the disappointment in her voice, she ran her finger around the rim of the bowl in which he was mixing lemon frosting.

Jeff tapped the back of her hand with the spoon handle. "Patience. When I'm finished, you can scrape the bowl."

She made a face. "I'm not sure I want to. That's really lemony. Is there anything else? I'm starving." With all that had gone on at lunch, she hadn't felt much like eating then.

He cut her a piece of unfrosted banana cake. "Will this hold you?"

She took a bite. It was still warm. "You ought to open a bakery," she said.

He laughed. "I have enough trouble keeping up with you and Eric." he said as he added more powdered sugar to the frosting.

Jennifer ate the cake slowly, savoring every bite. Trying to sound casual, she asked, "No one else called?"

"Just Steve," he said. Then he stopped stirring and looked at her, his head cocked to one side. "Who were you expecting?"

"Expecting?" *Hoping* would be a better word. "Oh, no one."

He looked skeptical.

She wondered if she should tell him about Tony. Maybe he could help her sort through the confusion.

By the time she'd gone to bed last night, she thought she had it worked out. It was just as Susan Hillard said at lunch: Coincidence; Tony walked her home because she happened to be there. Period.

She went over and over her conversation with Tony. He kept repeating, "You are really easy to talk to," in her head; each time he emphasized a different word. After a while, she couldn't remember exactly how he had said it. She settled on, "*You* are really easy to talk to." Would he have said that to just anybody?

Today with everybody teasing her and asking questions, she found herself back where she started — until Denise dropped her bombshell. Tony hadn't told her! More mixed feelings. On the one hand, she was relieved; on the other, she was disappointed.

Then when he smiled at her! It made her all quivery just thinking about it.

Eric burst into the kitchen. "Wait'll you hear what happened today!" He dropped his red backpack on the table. "Is the cake ready? Can I have a piece?"

Jeff put the finishing swirls on the icing. "It's all yours," he said.

"Really?" Eric said, his eyes wide. "The whole thing?"

"This whole piece," Jeff handed him a plate.

Eric was disappointed. "One piece?"

Jeff laughed. "That's the only way you can eat your cake and have it, too. At least until dessert tonight!" He settled down in the chair opposite Eric. "So let's hear it: What happened at school today?"

Jennifer gathered her books. Good thing Eric had come in when he did. She wasn't ready to tell Jeff what she was going through. Not yet. She had to sort some of it out herself. And maybe she could do that here where there was no one to badger her about Tony.

The telephone rang. Steve Crowley.

He told her there'd be meeting of the food committee for the hayride party tomorrow at lunch period. Then he said, "Hey, Jen, is there anything to this Tony thing?"

On her desk, her diary was still open to yesterday's page. *Today, Tony Hendrix walked me home.* She had gone to bed without adding another word.

Now, she sat down eagerly, ready to begin.

Dear Diary, You would not believe what I went through today! And all because Tony Hendrix walked me home yesterday. Tracy saw us together.

That last word brought her up short. "Together," she said aloud. She sat back to think about it. Did it imply a relationship? If Tony were to read it, what would he think? She crossed it out.

By lunchtime everyone knew. It was like that game of Telephone we used to play at parties. A whispered message is passed from one person to the next until the last person repeats it — except it's always different at the end. Today, no one whispered! But the message still got garbled along the way. Maybe that's because no one knows what the real message is — if there is one — not even me.

The clock downstairs chimed the half hour. She had to get moving. Tonight was her Save the Whales meeting. She had to finish her homework and call Nora before dinner.

She added, *Does anyone? Ever?*, closed the book and tucked it into her top drawer.

On the phone, Jennifer asked Nora, "Did Steve call you about the meeting?"

"Yeah, but I think he really called to talk about you and Tony," Nora said.

"He said something to you?"

"Mostly he asked questions."

"What did you tell him?"

"What you told me."

"I wonder if he called you before or after he called me."

"After," Nora said. "He said you wouldn't tell him anything."

Jennifer was exasperated. "I told him just what I told you."

"That's what I told him," Nora assured her. "But, you know, Jen, I think there's a lot more to it. You didn't tell me, and Tony didn't tell Denise. That's just the way we all acted over Mr. Rochester. Nobody told anybody anything!"

"That's because we were all crazy about

him," Jennifer said. "And we *did* tell Steve!"

Laughing, they remembered the disaster. Not only had Jennifer and Nora gone to Steve for advice on how to capture the attention of their teacher — everyone else had, too! He told them all the same things: cook for him; dress older. Each time, they carried out his ideas on the exact same day.

"The point is," Nora said, "we're best friends, and we didn't tell each other. Maybe a person keeps the really important things to herself."

Jennifer slid into her chair in the meeting room of the Cedar Groves Public Library at 8:05 P.M. Late again. This whole day had seemed like a race to catch up.

She had considered bypassing the meeting tonight. She hadn't finished her homework, and she had so much on her mind that she thought concentration would be difficult. But her interest in the group soon blocked out everything else.

At the end of the meeting, Conrad Matthews, president of the Save the Whales Association, talked about the possibility of sponsoring a fund raiser. He wanted suggestions, "But not now. Think about it until next time. That way we'll come up with a whale of an idea." He grinned and passed his hand over his bald head.

The poster of a blue whale tacked up on the cork board behind him made him seem especially small, like a Lilliputian beside Gulliver. But in this case, the man was out to free the giant, not capture it.

She was thinking about this contrast when she pushed through the library doors into the night air. It was a beautiful night, clear and bright.

From the shadows of the oak on the lawn, a voice said, "Hi, Jen. Save any whales tonight?"

Tony!

He stepped away from the tree and stood at the bottom of the stairs looking up at her. He'd had his hair cut.

After she said, "Hi," she didn't say anything for fear the words would stumble on her tongue.

"I was doing some research," he said, "and I saw you come in."

"I didn't see you," she said.

He laughed. "You looked pretty intent."

"I was late," she said. "I've been late all day long."

"I heard you had quite a day," he said.

Jennifer could feel herself redden. How could Denise tell him what she'd gone through today! She shifted from one foot to the other. "Well," she said without moving, "I'd better go."

"Is someone picking you up?" he asked.

"Jeff — he's our housekeeper."

"I know. Denise has told me about him."

Ms. Big Mouth, she thought and immediately dismissed it as small and unworthy. "He told me to call if I wanted a ride."

"How about if I walk you home?" Tony asked.

Not wanting to sound overly eager, she hesitated.

"If you don't want me to," he said, misinterpreting her silence, "I don't want to cause you any more trouble."

"Oh, it wasn't *trouble*," she assured him. "Just annoying." Smiling, she descended the stairs.

"What do you do at those meetings?" He asked as they crunched through the dry leaves on the library walk.

"Lots of things," she said. "Sometimes we write letters and we raise money. But mostly it's a matter of letting people know there is a problem."

"Do you think it does any good?"

"Oh, sure. If everyone got interested, things'd change."

"Everyone? That's expecting a lot, isn't it?"

On familiar territory — a cause she believed in — she felt herself relax. "But it's important. Do you realize there were two hundred thousand blue whales before nineteen-seventy and there're only six thousand five hundred now. Worldwide! And it's not just the whales: there're walrus, seals — lots of endangered animals. We have to do something about it because it affects all humanity."

"Lots of things do, Jen. There just isn't time."

"So much to do, so little time," she said.

He laughed. "Sounds like a slogan."

"It is." She opened her jacket to show him her T-shirt. She wore this one or one that said Save the Whales to every meeting. "Nora gave me this last Christmas."

"You're really serious, aren't you?" he said, admiration in his voice.

"A person has to be," she said.

"Have you ever seen a whale?" he asked.

"Not in person. Have you?"

"We were in California one year when they were migrating. I sat for hours with the binoculars watching for spouts. And then, there were those gigantic tails flipping up out of the water!"

"Some day I'm going to see them like that," Jennifer said.

Tony laughed. "Just don't get too close!"

"Oh, I want to. As close as I can."

"So did I," Tony said, "I had this romantic idea of them. All sleek and perfect.

Then we went out on a whale watch. What a disappointment!"

Jennifer was incredulous. "Why?"

"They're full of scars and —"

"Probably from harpoons," Jennifer said indignantly.

"And growths or something."

"Barnacles," Jennifer said.

"Whatever," Tony said. "All I know is they're not what I imagined."

"That doesn't mean we shouldn't do something to save them," Jennifer said, feeling her blood rise. "People can't go around killing things just because they're not perfect."

"Hold on, Jen," Tony said, laughing. "I'm with you." He raised his right hand. "Honest."

"Will you wear this?" She dug into her pocket and pulled out a Save the Whales pin.

"Proudly," he said, but when he went to pin it on, he stuck his finger. "If you pin it on."

She took the pin from his outstretched hand and reached up to attach it to his sweater. She hoped he didn't notice her hands trembling.

Chapter 6

Nora heard the phone ring in the distance, but she couldn't rouse herself. Earlier, when her mother had found her asleep at her desk, she had suggested Nora go to bed. Feeling fuzzy, Nora didn't need prodding.

Now, in her dreams, she was trying to connect with Jennifer, but things kept getting in the way — whales, people, skateboards — and Jennifer kept moving farther and farther away.

"Nora's asleep," Mrs. Ryan told Jennifer.

Jennifer was disappointed. The minute Tony had left, she'd rushed to the phone. She wanted to tell Nora about tonight before someone else did. More important, she needed to talk to her friend confidentially.

"She isn't sick, is she?" Jennifer asked.

"Just tired, I think," Nora's mother answered.

Jennifer was relieved. At least Nora would be in school. Hard as it would be, Jennifer would find a way to talk to her alone. For now, her diary would have to do. She got it out and opened it to that day's entry.

She rewrote *together* above the original word she had crossed out.

Jennifer left for school early hoping to catch Nora before everyone else got there. No such luck. Usually one of the first of their crowd to arrive, today Nora was the last.

"Where've you been?" Jennifer asked her. "I have to talk to you." Then she took a close look at her friend. "Nora, are you okay? You look strange."

"Not as strange as I feel," Nora said.

"What's the matter?"

"I don't know. Maybe something I ate."

"You should go home."

"I don't want to miss biology; it's lab day."

The bell rang.

"But if you're not feeling well. . . ."

Nora gave her friend a gentle push. "Come on, we'll be late."

Jennifer hesitated. "Are you sure?"

"Trust me," Nora said. "I'll be fine."

Jennifer's concern for her friend made her forget about Tony. Temporarily. But as she sat in homeroom waiting for Mr. Mario, who was late, it leaped into her mind: TONY! She couldn't risk saying anything here. Too many ears. She got out a piece of paper.

At the front of the room Jason and Mitch were shooting rubberbands at the map.

"Not the Adriatic Sea, you dope," Mitch said. "Italy! Let me show you."

"No you don't, Pauley," Jason protested. "It's still my turn."

Nora, Jennifer wrote, *Tony was at the library last night. He waited for me!*

Nora went to the back of the room to sharpen a pencil.

Jennifer couldn't put *this* note on Nora's desk. Someone else might get it. She tore it up and started over.

Guess who was at the library last night? Guess who waited for me? Guess who walked me home!

Someone said, "Here comes Mario!"

Mitch bolted to his place leaving Jason on his own.

Jennifer quickly folded the note and leaned across the aisle to put it on Nora's desk. In the scramble of people rushing to take their seats, she didn't see whether Nora got the note or not.

Trapped, Jason pretended to study the map while gathering the rubberbands with a foot. He stood on the pile with the other.

Mr. Mario swept in. He stopped short when he saw Jason.

" 'Morning, Mr. Mario," Jason said. "I was just . . . admiring your map."

Sighing his if-it's-not-one-thing-it's-another sigh, Mr. Mario inspected the map. "I don't suppose you noticed this hole?"

Jason looked horrified. "Hole? What hole?"

His back to Jason, the teacher said, "In Italy," as if it were a personal affront.

As Jason leaned down to scoop up the rubberbands, he threw Mitch a look that said, "Right on target." "No, sir," he said. "I didn't see any hole."

"Right here in the toe of the boot."

Jason stuffed the rubberbands in his pocket as he leaned in for a close look at the map. "That's a hole all right."

A couple of rubberbands fell out of his pocket. The class held its breath waiting for Mr. Mario to notice.

Mr. Mario reached for the tape on his desk. Then, as if struck by a sudden thought, he hesitated. He glanced around the room before fixing his gaze on Jason.

He knew!

Finally, he said, "Maybe we should call a shoemaker."

Jason was the first to laugh. "Toe of the boot. Shoemaker," he said. "That's a good one, Mr. Mario." Still laughing, he turned and started for his seat, leaving a trail of rubberbands behind him.

When the first period bell rang, Jennifer turned to Nora, but Denise got between them.

"Are you feeling all right?" Denise asked.

Nora smiled wanly. "Would you like to take my temperature?" she said — a joking reference to the day the eighth grade took over the school and Denise had been the nurse.

Jennifer was annoyed. Now there was no time to talk to Nora. And she certainly couldn't say anything in front of Denise. She'd repeat it to Tony.

Desperate, she whispered, "Did you get my note?" in Nora's ear as the three of them headed for their first period classes.

Nora didn't hear her.

People hovered over Nora all morning. Frustrating.

Nora didn't show up for lunch. Jennifer ate quickly and went looking for her. She found her friend in the girls' room examining her face in the mirror.

"Finally!" Jennifer said. "I've been looking all over for you. Did you eat?"

Groaning, Nora pulled down one lower eyelid and then the other.

"I have to talk to you," Jennifer said.

"As long as it isn't about food." Nora turned toward Jennifer and stuck out her tongue. She said, "Look at this! It's all coated," but it came out all garbled and Jennifer didn't understand a word.

Mia came in. She sprayed gold glitter in her green hair and added a fresh coat of black lipstick. Moving close to Nora, she said. "Lookin' good. My hair and your face." Then she breezed out.

Nora looked horrified. "Green! Do I look *green*?"

"Not exactly green," Jennifer said. "More like chartreuse."

"Gross me out!" Nora said.

"Maybe you should go home," Jennifer suggested.

Nora gathered her things. "After biology." She started for the door. "Come on. We're late for Steve's meeting."

"Oh, no," Jennifer said. "I forgot about that."

Her head down so that no one could see how awful she looked, Nora led the way to the classroom where the meeting was to be held. At the door, she got behind Jennifer. "Who's in there?"

Jennifer looked through the window in the door. "Steve," she said. "And Joan Wesley."

Nora moaned. Joan had been cafeteria

manager when they took over the school. She had been on Nora's case the whole day.

Knowing what her friend was thinking, Jennifer added, "Steve thinks she has good organizational skills. He doesn't know it's spelled b-o-s-s-y."

Nora started to laugh but it doubled her over. "Owww," she moaned.

"Where does it hurt?" Jennifer asked.

"Everywhere," Nora answered.

Steve saw Jennifer's face at the window and came to open the door. "Thought you'd forgotten," he said.

Inside, Nora sank into the nearest chair and put her head on the desk.

"Everyone here?" Jennifer asked.

"Still one missing, but he'll be along." Steve consulted his clipboard. "We got started without you."

Nora raised her head. "Then we can leave?"

"We haven't decided anything yet," Steve said. "I thought chili" — A shiver shot through Nora. — "might be a good choice, but — "

Nora said, "Chili."

"We can't take a vote until we have all the suggestions," Joan said. "And I suggest hot dogs" — Nora's stomach lurched. — "because everyone can roast their own and they're easier to eat."

Nora repeated, "Hot dogs."

Joan was exasperated. "Make up your mind, Nora."

Brad Hartley flung open the door. "Sorry I'm late."

Nora felt the color drain out of her face. She raised her head slightly. There Brad stood with his broad shoulders and fantastic smile looking so handsome and so *healthy*. Nora couldn't stand it. "Brad Hartley," she said.

"Are you okay, Nora?" he asked. "You look so pale."

Better than chartreuse, she thought.

As he moved to take the place beside her, she pushed herself up out of her chair. "I think I'm going to be — " Her hands cupped over her mouth, she ran for the door.

Behind her, Brad said, "What'd I say?"

Biology was disaster. Between worrying about Nora and thinking about Tony, Jennifer was all thumbs; Mr. Morris kept stopping at their table to check progress, of which there was none; and Steve kept staring at her.

With all the unwanted attention, Jennifer broke two eggs preparing for an osmosis experiment.

Finally, Denise said, "Why don't you fill the beaker, Jen, and I'll get the egg ready."

Jennifer had just filled the container

when Steve said at her elbow, "What's wrong, Jen?"

As she wheeled to face him, the water sloshed all over. "Now look what you made me do," she snapped, instantly regretting it.

Steve grabbed a rag and mopped up the mess. "Sorry, I didn't mean to startle you."

"Don't pay any attention to me, Steve," she said. "I'm kinda edgy."

"That's for sure! Is anything wrong?"

"Nora's sick."

"That's what wrong with Nora; what's wrong with you?" He studied her with his knowing blue eyes.

Avoiding his steady gaze, she reached for a paper towel to wipe off her rubber lab apron. "I'm not good at this," she said referring to the class. "Nora usually does the actual work. Denise and I do the reports."

She could tell he didn't believe her, but he didn't say anything. Instead, he stepped back toward his place. "If you need any help, just whistle."

With the period nearly over and not much accomplished, Denise said, "We'll have to come back after school to finish."

"Can't," Jennifer said. "It's my afternoon at the nursing home."

"What about over the weekend?"

Denise suggested. "You could come to my house."

Tony's house! As tempting as that sounded, Jennifer wasn't sure she could handle it. "Or mine," she offered.

Denise shook her head. "Mine'd be better. Tony's good in biology. He could help us."

Jennifer's heart shifted into double-time. "Would he want to?" she asked, tentatively adding, "I mean . . . well, you said he's so depressed and everything."

"He seems better," Denise said. "He's still moping around, but at least he's not following me everywhere wanting to talk. I suppose he's boring someone else with the whole thing. Anyway, it'd do him good to help us. Take his mind off things."

Jennifer was soaring when she left school. *She* was the one Tony had chosen to talk to. And it was far from boring!

As she flew by the high school on her way to the nursing home, she collided with a group of girls.

The smallest of them looked up at Jennifer, her violet eyelids blinking furiously. "Grow up!" she snapped.

Jessica Hartnett!

From where she stood looking down into Jessica's violet eyes, Jennifer suddenly felt very small.

Chapter 7

Jennifer phoned Nora as soon as she returned from the nursing home. She let it ring twelve times.

"No one's there," she told Jeff, alarm in her voice. "Maybe Nora's in the hospital."

"Or sleeping," Jeff said.

"But her mother'd answer."

"Not if she went back to work."

Jennifer hadn't thought of that. Mrs. Ryan had picked Nora up at school. She might have taken her home, gotten her settled and returned to her Legal Aid office.

Jennifer decided to check. "I think I'll take Nora's assignments over."

"Take Eric with you," Jeff suggested. "He has to go to the library."

Jennifer understood. A fourth-grader, Eric was old enough to go alone, but without someone there to remind him of the time, he'd stay until closing.

"Don't forget you came to do homework," Jennifer reminded her brother as he headed for the rack of Choose-Your-Own-Adventure books. "I'll be back in half an hour." Eric was already in another world.

Outside the library, Jason Anthony was lying in wait. He had seen Jennifer and her little brother go in and decided to ambush them. When Jennifer came out alone, he didn't know what to do. He liked Jennifer. She was always kind even when she called him names. And the last couple of days she had become suddenly mysterious as though she had a secret. Fascinating. And scary.

Before he knew what he was doing, he was sneaking up on her. With several yards to go, he took a running start, passed her, dropped his skateboard, and jumped on, all in one smooth motion.

"Oh, Jason!" Jennifer exclaimed. "You scared me."

"Bomb drop," Jason said, explaining the maneuver.

Jennifer laughed. "That's what it sounds like."

He tic-tacked along beside her. "There's

a lot more to skateboarding than most people realize."

Jennifer wasn't in the mood to hear about the fine points of skateboarding, but she didn't want to hurt Jason's feelings. "You'll have to tell me about it sometime," she said.

"How about right now?" he asked, surprising himself. "I'll even show you some basic moves."

"I haven't time now, Jason. I have to go over to Nora's."

"Thought she was sick."

"She is. That's why."

"I'll go along. Maybe she could use some cheering up."

"That's really nice, Jason, but she's probably not up to it."

He shrugged. "So I'll go along anyway. Keep you company."

Now he'd done it. What would he talk about all the way to Nora's? Worse, what if Jennifer told him to buzz off?

He pushed off and sailed ahead of her. He turned to smile at her, his red hair a bright halo in the late afternoon sun.

He wasn't so bad — not when he was away from the other boys and didn't show off as much. Jennifer remembered how he'd disappeared during their Washington trip not long before. When they'd finally found him at the bus station, he confessed that he was homesick. That had touched Jennifer. She had thought then as she did now that people's insides don't always match their outsides.

As she approached, he hopped off the skateboard, tipped it up with his foot, and stashed it under his arm. Then, he ducked behind a bush. Now what was he playing?

Jennifer walked past his hiding place without looking back. Suddenly, she felt a spray of ice cold water. She wheeled around. There stood Jason aiming a hose right at her.

"You creep!" she exploded. "Why don't you grow up!" She turned on her heel and stalked off.

Jason laughed maniacally. "Hey, Jen!" he called after her. "Anyone ever tell you you're all wet?" Of himself he thought, *Anthony, you are really a creep.*

"Creep!" Jennifer said above the sound of the hair dryer.

Nora made a muffled sound of agreement from the comfort of her bed.

"Just when I was thinking he was okay, he goes and does a stupid thing like this!" Jennifer went on.

Nora coughed.

"Someone ought to *do* something about him!"

Nora cleared her throat.

"Teach him how to behave or something!"

Nora reached for the tissue box on her nightstand.

"He's a menace!"

Nora blew her nose.

"There should be laws against people like him!"

Nora yawned.

"He should be locked up!"

Nora closed her eyes.

Jennifer turned off the hair dryer and leaned close to Nora's mirror. The dousing Jason had given her had temporarily submerged her need to talk to Nora about Tony, but now that she had expressed her anger, it came bobbing to the surface. She decided to lead into it slowly. After all the energy she'd spent trying to convince everyone there was nothing between her and Tony, her abrupt about-face was bound to be a shock, especially when Nora wasn't feeling well.

She pulled her long dark hair up so that it was the same length as Jessica Hartnett's, with the ends just brushing her ears. "Maybe I should cut my hair," she said.

Nora didn't respond.

Jennifer let her hair fall back around her shoulders and shook her head. "No. I like it like this. Why should I cut it? But

I really need a change." She studied her hazel eyes. "My eyes maybe." The dark liner she'd applied this morning was worn off. "What I should do is wear more eye makeup. Violet or something colorful." She fluttered her eyelids. "Tracy said I should do that. At the beginning of the year. Remember? Violet, she said, with frosty pearl just here under the brow line. That might look really good. Bring out my eyes."

Nora was silent.

Still studying her image, Jennifer said, "Nora? Did you get my note this morning?" She turned to face her friend.

Nora was asleep.

After supper, Jennifer picked up the phone to call Denise. What if Tony answers? She put down the receiver. Denise was her friend, wasn't she? The only way she could avoid the possibility of Tony's answering was never to call. What would Denise think then? She picked up the receiver and dialed the first three numbers. She hesitated. What if Tony answers and thinks I'm calling him? He'll think I'm chasing him!

A mechanical voice said, "We're sorry. We can't complete your call as dialed. Please hang up and try again."

"No, thanks," Jennifer said aloud as she

replaced the receiver. Denise'd probably call her. After all, she'd been the one to suggest they do their biology lab work at her house.

Jennifer went downstairs to talk to Jeff. He was in the family room watching an old movie with his friend, Debby Kincaid.

Debby smiled when Jennifer entered. Under the soft light from the lamp beside her, she looked much younger than the forty plus Jennifer knew her to be. Debby had to be at least ten years younger than Jeff. Jennifer'd never thought about that before. It hadn't seemed important. But now —

"Jennifer?" Debby said.

She must have been staring.

"You okay?" Jeff asked.

"Fine," Jennifer assured them both. "Just wondered what everyone was doing."

"My Friday night vice," Debby said. "Old movies and popcorn."

"Hey," Jeff protested. "How about me?"

Debby laughed. "I'm glad you're here, too!"

Jennifer liked seeing them together. They had such a sense of fun. Sometimes, she imagined her mother and father teasing one another in a similar way.

"Popcorn?" Jeff asked as he held out the bowl.

"Maybe later," Jennifer said. "Right now I have to make a phone call."

"Hello."

Tony!

Jennifer covered the mouthpiece with her hand and took a deep breath.

"Hello?" Tony said again. His voice was rich and deep.

"Is Denise there?" Jennifer asked. Maybe he wouldn't recognize her voice.

"Jen?"

She swallowed. "Tony? Hi. Is Denise there? I have to talk to her about — " She couldn't say *homework*; it sounded so dumb. " — something."

"Boys?" he teased.

That sounded even dumber!

"Biology. Nora usually does the lab work and then I do the drawings and Denise fills in the reports. Only Nora got sick today and had to go home and then I broke two eggs during an osmosis experiment and — " She knew she was rattling on, but couldn't seem to stop. She was relieved when Tony broke in.

"Nora? Sick?" he said. "What happened to her 'preventive medicine'?"

Jennifer tried to think of a clever comeback, but she couldn't. Instead, she laughed.

She heard Denise's muffled voice saying, "Give me the phone, Tony."

"Just a minute, Denise," Tony said. "I'm not finished."

"But it's for me," Denise said in the background.

"Jen? Who'd you rather talk to: Denise or me?" Tony's voice faded.

"Hi, Jen," Denise said into the phone. "I apologize for my brother."

For what? Jennifer wondered. "Oh, that's okay," she said.

"What about tomorrow?" Denise asked her. "Can you come over?"

"I have to go to the animal shelter in the morning," Jennifer said, "but after that — "

"Great. Come as soon as you can. Listen, I gotta go. Talk to you tomorrow."

A click and Denise was gone. But not Tony. Tony's voice was echoing in her head. *Jen?* It sounded special the way he said it.

Chapter 8

The Hendrixes' doorbell chimed "Strawberry Fields Forever."

Jennifer pulled at her skirt as she waited for someone to answer. She had agonized over what to wear all last night. She didn't have time to go home to change between work at the animal shelter and coming here. And she had to look just right. Before she went to bed, she'd decided on her red shaker knit sweater and the faded Guess jeans. Then, this morning, it struck her: Jessica Hartnett always wore skirts. She started all over again, pulling everything out of her closet. Finally, she'd put on this black skirt and the oversized peach flat knit sweater. A mistake: The skirt was uncomfortably short even for desk duty at the animal shelter. Of course, it could have been worse; she might have been assigned work in the kennels.

She heard someone coming. Tony? Her heart beat wildly.

When Denise opened the door, Jennifer heard the muffled voice of Bruce Springsteen singing.

"Denise!" Jennifer said.

Denise laughed. "You sound surprised."

Jennifer recovered quickly. "I am! I always expect a butler or someone to open your door." To an extent, that was true. The Hendrixes' three-story stone house set on twenty acres of rolling hillside was one of Cedar Groves' few mansions. Until Denise moved in, Jennifer had never been in a house so grand.

Denise stepped back, bowed, and ushered Jennifer inside with a sweep of her arm. "Ms. Hendrix is expecting you," she said in her most formal tone. *"Entré-vous."*

Jennifer took a deep breath, said, *"Merci,"* and stepped into the house, looking around as if this were her first time in it.

As Denise led the way to the large blue and white kitchen, Jennifer glanced into the open rooms along the way. The music was loudest outside the den door, which was closed.

"I've already done the egg," Denise said.

Jennifer inspected the experiment. A water-filled eggshell rested in a hole cut in the center of a cardboard square placed over a container of water. "Did you remember the salt?" she asked.

"Uh-huh. And I added blue food coloring so the crystals'll show up better when they osmose. Is that a word?" Without waiting for an answer, Denise continued, "While we're waiting for it to do that, you could draw the setup, and I'll start the report."

Jennifer opened her bookbag on the table and took out her notebook.

"Let's work in the den," Denise said.

Jennifer hesitated. She was sure Tony was in that room. "I thought I heard someone in there."

"It's only Tony. He likes the stereo in there better than his." Denise started out of the kitchen. "Besides, he told me he'd help."

Jennifer tagged along behind her, taking deep breaths. Except for their footsteps, there was no sound. Tony had turned off the music. Was he still there behind the closed door?

Denise knocked and opened the den door in one motion.

Stretched out on a section of the white couch that snaked around the room, bright silk pillows behind his head, Tony was staring at the beams of the cathedral ceiling when the girls entered. He didn't seem to be aware of them.

"Don't let us disturb you," Denise said.

"Wha — ?" he said, and then he scrambled to his feet, smiling past his sister at Jennifer. He was wearing the Save the Whales pin on his striped rugby shirt.

She had forgotten hers. She hoped he didn't notice.

"Hi," he said.

Jennifer could feel herself redden. Fortunately, Denise was busy clearing off the game table near the windows.

"Hi," Jennifer said, returning his smile.

"We got the experiment set up," Denise said. "And we can't do anything much about that until it does what it's supposed to do — *if* it does what it's supposed to. But we have these problems you could help us with. Mr. Morris *loves* problems. He's always giving them. Except when we were dissecting pigs. He said that was problem enough. Sometimes, I wish we were still dissecting pigs." She gave that thought. "I guess that's going too far." She looked at Jennifer. "Jen, do you have the problems?"

Like a lagging computer, Jennifer's mind was a sentence or two behind Denise. When she caught up, she tore her gaze away from Tony and put her bookbag on the table. "I remember one," she said as she fumbled through her science folder. " 'There are two containers. In the first is one cell. In the second are two. It takes each cell three minutes to divide. If it takes the two cells three hours to fill the container, how long will it take one?' "

Denise said, "I don't remember that one at all," as she flipped through her notebook.

"Sounds more like math than biology," Tony said.

Jennifer glanced over her science notes. The puzzle she'd just quoted was not there. Feeling foolish, she said, "It *is* a math problem." she smiled sheepishly. "Sorry about that."

"Do you know the answer?" Tony asked her.

"Easy," Denise said. "Six hours."

"You sure?" he asked his sister.

"Absolutely," Denise said. "If it takes one cell three hours, it'll take two twice as long — six hours."

"What'd you think, Jen?" he asked.

Jennifer hesitated. Six hours was the obvious answer — too obvious. That's why she thought it was wrong. But she hated to say so in front of Tony and take the risk of appearing really dumb. "Well," she began. "Denise could be right, but I think the answer's three hours and three minutes."

"That can't be right," Denise said. "How can that be right?"

Tony beamed, admiration in his eyes. "Jen?" he said. "Why don't you explain it to her."

His conspiratorial tone made Jennifer feel very smart.

"I don't know how I could be so dumb!" Nora said to her sister Sally. "To get sick like that right in front of Brad Hartley."

Sally finished her salad and took her plate to the sink. "More soup?" she asked Nora.

Nora shook her head. Although she was feeling much better, her appetite was still not up to par. "One cup of chicken soup and I'm totally full."

"That's an improvement," Sally reminded her.

True. Yesterday, even the *thought* of food had nauseated her. "Did you know chicken soup really works? There's something in it that helps relieve cold and flu symptoms. Even medical people recognize its effects."

"Maybe it's the TLC that goes with it," Sally suggested as she stuffed her ballet shoes into her duffel bag.

"There's more to it than that."

"As long as it works," Sally said.

Thinking of Brad Hartley, Nora said, "That's the problem. I'll probably be well by Monday and then what'll I do?"

"Be thankful," Sally said. She zipped up her bag and adjusted her leg warmers.

"I mean about Brad," Nora explained

patiently. "I'll see him at school."

At the door Sally said, "And he'll see you," and then she was gone.

"A lot of help you are," Nora called after her.

She looked at the clock. Jen should be home from the animal shelter by now. She'd give her a call. Together they could figure out how Nora should approach Brad after their disastrous meeting yesterday.

Eric answered the phone. "Jen's not here," he told Nora. "I don't know where she is."

Nora heard Jeff Crawford's voice in the background.

"Jeff says she's at Denise's," Eric said.

"What's she doing there?" Nora asked.

"How should I know?" Eric said. "Bye." He hung up.

Nora was annoyed. Why didn't Jen tell her she was going to Denise's today? Was she trying to keep it from her? Ridiculous, she assured herself. She knew better than to think Denise could come between them. They'd been all through that at the beginning of the year when Denise first arrived. Then, Jennifer recognized Denise's loneliness and included her. Nora had admired Jennifer for her kindness; at the same time she felt their friendship was in danger. As Nora got to know and like Denise, she realized that it had been a threat only because she let it be. Still, as she hung up the phone, she felt left out. Because she wasn't feeling well, she decided.

Jen would probably stop over later. Nora would talk to her then. In the meantime, she'd go upstairs and get into bed with a good book.

Denise had never felt more left out, not even during those first days at Cedar Groves Junior High. Then, even though her classmates ignored her, they knew she was there. Tony and Jennifer hardly seemed aware that she was in the room.

They had gotten off the biology problem solving and gone on to unexplained animal behavior.

"No one knows why whales beach themselves," Jennifer was saying.

"The answer's probably too simple for experts," Tony said.

"It's like sharks," Jennifer continued. "They rub their backs along the bottom of the ocean or on coral or something. No one can figure that out, either."

"They probably itch," Tony said.

Jennifer raised her arms as though she were about to lead a cheer. "That's what I think!" she exclaimed.

Tony smiled. "Great minds . . ." he said.

Denise couldn't stand it another minute. She slammed her noteboook shut and stood up. "Great minds might run on the *same* track," she said, finishing the cliché Tony had left dangling, "but that doesn't mean it's the *right* track." She stormed out of the room.

Amused, Tony watched after her. Then, he looked at Jennifer and, with mock seriousness, said, "She may have a point there."

Jennifer giggled.

Shortly after the telephone rang, Denise returned.

"It's for you," she said to her brother, adding, "A girl," with obvious emphasis.

Tony was certain she'd done that for Jennifer's benefit.

"I'll take it in the kitchen," he said as he crossed to the door, where he turned and smiled. "See you, Jen."

He wondered what was eating Denise. The only other times he'd seen her act like this was when he brought Jessica to the house. At first he had thought she was jealous, but it soon became clear that Jessica and Denise disliked one another. Why Denise had acted as she had in front of Jennifer was a mystery. Jen was her friend. He was just being nice.

Chapter 9

"It's not working," Denise told Jennifer. "There aren't any crystals on the egg-shell."

Jennifer shifted the phone to her other ear. "Maybe you haven't given it enough time."

"No, Jen, that's not it. I did something wrong. I know I did. Could you come over and take a look at it?"

"Sure. Give me a few minutes to get dressed." Tony might be there! What would she wear? It would take her longer than a few minutes to decide. "How's one?"

"That's two hours!" Denise exclaimed. "Couldn't you get here before that? If we don't get this set up right soon, we'll never have the results in time."

"I'll be there as soon as I can," Jennifer assured her.

Jeff Crawford glanced up from the Arts section of the Sunday newspaper. "Crisis?"

"Biology experiment. Denise goofed it up." Jennifer snatched a sweet roll and made for the door. "I don't know what to wear."

"It shouldn't matter unless you're up for the Nobel prize," Jeff said.

Something better than that, Jennifer thought as she raced up the stairs two at a time. In her room, she leaned against her door mentally ticking off the clothes in her closet. She couldn't start dragging them all out again; she'd just gotten them put away. And Denise was probably pacing the floor waiting for her. She opened her closet. There wasn't a thing in it that appealed to her. Everything, except the green outfit her father had bought, was so babyish. And she couldn't wear that; she'd worn it the day Tony walked her home from school. Finally, her sense of responsibility won out over her desire to please Tony. She pulled on the Guess jeans and red sweater she'd vetoed yesterday.

Just as she was going out the door, the phone rang.

Nora.

"Can I call you later?" Jennifer asked her. "I'm on my way to Denise's."

"Don't let me keep you," Nora said and hung up. "Some friend," she said to the empty kitchen. "She didn't even ask how I am."

Jennifer sighed. Nora could be difficult sometimes. She'd call her later and explain. Now, she had to hurry.

As she sailed out of the house, Jeff called after her, "Remember, your father's coming home today."

Tony answered the door.

"You look terrific," he told her. "Red's great on you."

"Thanks," she said. She wanted to say he looked great himself, but she was afraid he'd think it was an automatic response. Besides, he must know he looked wonderful. He always did. "Denise around?"

"In the kitchen clucking over an egg."

A literal picture of that description popped into Jennifer's head. She laughed.

Denise came out to greet her. "Am I glad you're here!"

Jen followed her back into the kitchen. Tony tagged along behind, stopping just inside the doorway where he leaned against the wall and folded his arms across his chest.

"Don't you have somewhere to go?" Denise asked him.

His dark eyes twinkled. "It can wait."

"We don't need your help," Denise snapped.

"I'm not offering it," Tony teased her.

Exasperated, Denise turned her attention to the egg. "What do you think, Jen?"

"Nothing's happening," Jennifer said.

"I know that!" Denise said. "What do we do about it?"

Jennifer was aware of Tony watching her. It was unnerving. She reached for the egg, then drew back her hand. What if she broke it? He'd think she was a real klutz. "You put in the salt?" she asked Denise.

"You asked me that yesterday," Denise said.

"Right," Jennifer said. Then she didn't say anything.

Finally, Denise said, "So what could be wrong?"

Jennifer shook her head.

Denise reached for the egg. "Let's just dump this and start over."

Struck by a sudden idea, Jennifer told her to wait. "*Where*'d you put the salt?"

"In the water," Denise said.

"Which water?" Jennifer asked. "In the eggshell or under it?"

Denise thought about that. "Where's it belong?"

"In the eggshell."

"Then that's where I put it."

"You're sure?"

"No," Denise admitted. "I don't remember where I put it."

Jennifer dipped her finger into the eggshell and tasted the water. Then she lifted the cardboard on which it rested and tasted the water in the measuring cup. She made a face.

"I'll bet I know where you put it," Tony said.

Denise threw the eggshell at him as he ducked out of the room.

She and Jennifer were putting the experiment back together when Nora called.

"Can I call you back later?" Denise asked her. "Jen and I are in the middle of something."

Nora was miffed. She hadn't heard from Jennifer all day yesterday. And today, she and Denise were so busy they couldn't talk to her. What could possibly be that important? Neither one of them had even asked whether she was better. Obviously, this was a case of out of sight, out of mind. She'd show them.

She dialed Lucy Armanson.

"Lucy's with Amy and Tracy," Mrs. Armanson said. "I'll tell her you called."

"Never mind," Nora said. "It's not important."

Jessica Ryan came into the kitchen for a glass of water. Looking over her reading glasses, she asked her daughter, "What's the matter?"

Nora said, "Get sick and you're dead!" and stormed out of the room.

Sitting cross-legged on Denise's Laura Ashley chintz bedspread, Jennifer said hesitantly, "You put on eye makeup so well." Jennifer thought Denise used more makeup than her other friends, except Mia, but she applied it so skillfully, it was difficult to detect. And, unlike Jennifer and Nora, Denise never talked about it.

Denise shrugged and nodded, saying, "When your parents are in the business . . ." as though she had no choice in the matter.

Jennifer said, "Whenever I put it on, I look like Mia. Or Andy!"

Denise laughed. "Andy's into punk makeup, and Mia knows exactly what she's doing."

"But I don't know what I'm doing, and it shows, so I don't bother."

"Want me to show you?" Denise was already at her dressing table.

"Would you?"

Denise opened a drawer. It was filled with Denise Cosmetics of every description organized in a large plastic tray. Denise nodded toward the skirted stool fronting the table. Dutifully, Jennifer sat down.

"Think of your face as a canvas," Denise

said. "You're the artist." She tried various foundation colors on Jennifer's skin, finally deciding on a warm peachy-beige. She wiped Jennifer's face clean of the sample colors and applied her choice evenly with a small sponge. Next, she applied a rosy blush with a black-bristled brush.

When she got to the eyes, Denise took out a palette of colorful eye shadow squares. "You have beautiful eyes, Jen," she said. "You could wear brown, green — almost any color."

"Violet?" Jennifer asked eagerly.

"Violet'd be great if you weren't wearing a red sweater." Denise looked over the rainbow of colors. "Let's try strawberry with canary."

Jennifer envisioned herself with red and yellow eyelids. "It'll look like someone hit me!"

"Trust me," Denise said. "The secret is in the blending."

Jennifer was so engrossed in her friend's every move she didn't see her image changing in the dressing table mirror. When Denise said, "Voilà!" Jennifer looked into large, hazel eyes that returned her astonished gaze.

Her breath caught. Wishing Tony were still home to see the transformation, she said, "Is that me?"

Denise laughed. "You were expecting someone else?"

Willie Nelson and Jeff Crawford were singing "You Were Always on My Mind" when Jennifer burst into the kitchen.

"Dad home yet?" she asked.

Jeff glanced at her, shook his head, and looked away. Suddenly, stopping his song midword, he did a double take. A whistle escaped the cage of his teeth as he reached back to snap off the radio. "Wait until your father sees you!" he said.

"Think he'll like it?" She turned her head to the side and tipped up her chin.

"If I remember correctly," he said. "a pretty girl named Jennifer Mann left here a couple of hours ago."

She turned full face. "He won't like it."

"And now, a *beautiful* girl named Jennifer Mann has returned."

She curbed the instinct to hug him. Displays of affection flustered him. Instead, she smiled broadly, "Beautiful? Really?"

He smiled. "Enchanting. Couldn't be you've had another dose of that sunshine you mentioned the other day?"

"Could be," she said, smiling enigmatically. "Anyone call?"

"Nora. Twice."

Jennifer wasn't anxious to return the

calls. She knew Nora was upset, and she was feeling too good herself to deal with it. But if she didn't do it now, she might not have another chance.

"Hi, Nora," she said when Nora answered. "How're you feeling?"

It's about time, Nora thought. She said, "Better."

"Think you'll be in school tomorrow?"

Why? You and Denise planning something you'd rather do without me? "If I feel as good as I do today," Nora said.

"Great! I miss you."

She sounded as though she really meant it. Softening, Nora said, "I miss you, too."

"Biology sure isn't the same without you," Jennifer said. "Denise and I really blew it Friday."

Biology? Nora thought. Denise and I? She said nothing.

She's still upset, Jennifer thought. Anxious to patch things up, she rattled on. "We spent yesterday doing an experiment we messed up in class, and today we had to start all over again, because Denise goofed. We did it at her house, because Tony" — How she loved to say his name! — "offered to help. He's good in biology. Not as good as you, but good." She trailed off. She wanted to tell Nora about Tony and her feelings for him but not over the phone. "So anyway, we'll finish the experiment, and you won't have to worry about making it up or anything."

Nora noted a sudden change in Jennifer's voice. It was as though she'd lost her train of thought or was thinking something other than what she was saying. She probably realizes she's hurt my feelings, Nora thought. I'm being too hard on her. "Maybe we could do something after school tomorrow," she said.

"Great! I'm dying to talk to you."

Nora was about to hang up when she remembered, "My scarf! Will you remind me to get it? Sally wanted to borrow it last night, and I looked all over for it before I remembered Mr. Mario had it."

"Did you patch things up?" Jeff asked as Jennifer hung up.

She wasn't surprised Jeff knew there was trouble. He often seemed to sense what was going on.

"I hope so," she said.

"Relationships don't grow without trouble," he said.

"You and Debby don't seem to have any problems," she said.

He laughed. "We have our moments."

Now was her chance to talk to him about Tony without mentioning names. "Debby's a lot younger than you, isn't she?"

" 'A lot'?" Jeff's expression was mock horror. "Just what do you mean by 'a lot'?"

"Ten years?" Jennifer asked tentatively.

"Please," Jeff said.

"How many then?"

"I'm not actually sure. Debby believes her age is a sacred trust never to be revealed."

"But you *are* older?"

"Unfortunately."

"You mean it's a problem? The age difference?"

"Between us? No. Only for me."

"Because she's younger?"

"Because I'm older."

Jennifer was puzzling through that one when her father opened the back door.

"Anybody home?" he said.

Jennifer ran to him and threw her arms around his neck.

Laughing, he returned her hug. "Careful," he said. "You'll knock me off my feet." He held her at arm's length and studied her as though he were seeing her for the first time.

"I have the feeling it won't be too long before she's knocking lots of people off their feet," Jeff put in.

Mr. Mann didn't seem to hear him.

"You're getting to look more like your mother every day," he said, and then he pulled her close for another hug. Finally, he patted her on the back and turned to pick up his suitcase. "So. What did I interrupt?"

"We were discussing May — December relationships," Jeff said. He reconsidered. "Make that July — October."

"I was wondering if it's a problem between people; a difference in age," Jennifer clarified.

"Between a man and a woman you mean," her father said.

"Or . . . a boy and a girl," Jennifer said hesitantly. She hoped he wouldn't ask her which boy and girl.

Mr. Mann looked at Jeff. "Any coffee?" Setting his suitcase on the floor beside him, he sat down at the table. "Your mother was younger than I."

Jennifer eased into the chair opposite him. "I didn't know that."

Jeff brought his employer a steaming cup and discreetly left the room.

"Did I ever tell you about our shadows?" her father asked.

"Shadows?" He seemed to have forgotten about the age difference. But that was all right. He seldom talked about her mother and when Jennifer asked about her, his face would cloud over and he'd say, "What's past is past." Now, he was not only willing but eager to talk about her.

"I was remembering that driving home.

The way the light is, I suppose," he said.

"Tell me," Jennifer said eagerly.

"She said they matched — our shadows. We were walking along the beach arm in arm, and she drew my attention to our shadows stretched out in front of us. 'They match,' she said. They didn't. Not exactly. I was taller, but they looked good together as though they belonged side by side." He paused lingering on this memory. "Your mother turned to me then and said, 'Yes.' I knew what she meant — I'd been asking her to marry me for months — but I didn't know until years later that I had our shadows to thank for her answer."

As romantic as that sounded, Jennifer's practical side was reluctant to accept it. "She decided to marry you just because your shadows matched?"

"She had already decided to say 'yes', but this . . . thing with the shadows clinched it." He looked at Jennifer silently for several seconds. Then he stood up suddenly. "Stay right where you are." He picked up his suitcase. "I didn't have time to buy anything for you this trip but — "

"You don't have to buy me anything," Jennifer interrupted.

"Just stay put." He crossed to the hall door. "I'll be right back. I have something special for you."

Jennifer watched after him thinking

nothing could be more special than what he'd just given her.

Dear Diary, Today was a perfect day. Denise and I did an experiment at her house. Tony was there. He is soooooo nice. And soooooo handsome. When he smiles at me, I feel all warm and wonderful. Denise showed me how to put on makeup so it looks natural, only better. And my father gave me my mother's gold locket.

Jennifer drew a heart, the shape of her new locket. Then she wrote: *Inside, there's a small picture of the two of them on their wedding day. Dad says I look like her. I sure hope so; she was beautiful.*

She reread the entry. In her empty heart drawing, she added:

J. M.
+
T. H.

Chapter 10

Mitch Pauley leaned against his gym locker waiting for Tommy Ryder to finish changing. "What's with Mann?" he asked.

Tommy Ryder shook his head. "Beats me. She sure seems different."

"I noticed that last week at the library," Jason put in.

Tommy Ryder looked up at him from the bench where he was tying his shoe. "You saw Jennifer Mann at the library?"

It sounded like an accusation.

"So what?" Jason said defensively.

"When?" Tommy persisted.

"I don't know. Last week, Friday, I think. I waited for her and — "

Tommy rose slowly. "You *waited* for her?"

Jason backed off. "Well, yeah. Sort of."

"Did you walk her home?"

Jason responded with a noncommittal shrug.

"That's it!" Tommy concluded.

"That's what?" Mitch asked.

"Take a look at this!" Tommy dug in his jeans pocket and pulled out a crumpled piece of paper. He handed it to Mitch. "Read that!"

Mitch's lips moved as he read the note. Then, he shook his head. "I don't get it."

"Let me see," Jason said.

Tommy ignored him. "Whose handwriting is it?"

Mitch took another look. The *i*'s were dotted with small circles. Mitch shrugged.

"Give me that!" Jason snatched the note. " '*Guess who was at the library last night?*'," he read. " '*Guess who waited for me? Guess who walked me home!*' " He looked up. "Jennifer wrote this note," he said. "Where'd you get it?"

"I picked it up with the paper airplanes before Mario got to homeroom this morning," Tommy explained. "It was partway under the radiator."

"It says 'last night,' " Mitch said. "The library's not open on Sunday nights."

"She probably wrote it Friday," Tommy said.

Mitch was more confused. "Jason said he saw her on Friday."

Jason reread the note to himself. It was Friday, he was sure of it. The mistake must have been Jennifer's. She probably wrote it this morning. In her excitement, she got confused.

Tommy and Mitch were looking at him.

He smiled sheepishly. "Thursday, Friday — whenever."

"And he walked her home," Tommy said. "It all fits."

Jason didn't dispute that. If he hadn't actually walked her home, he'd offered to. That part must be Jennifer's wishful thinking.

"That explains everything!" Tommy said.

"What everything?" Mitch asked.

"Jennifer's in love!"

Mitch glared at Tommy. He felt as though the quarterback was calling the plays without giving the players the numbers. "With *Jason?*"

Jennifer fingered her new locket. Denise had noticed it this morning as she had Jennifer's makeup.

"You were right about the violet eye shadow," she said.

Jennifer'd gotten up an hour early to try to reproduce the effect Denise had achieved yesterday. It hadn't been easy. Her eyes kept watering; she couldn't control the eye liner; the mascara streaked; the blush wouldn't blend. She nearly gave up. In the end, she was glad she hadn't.

"But no one noticed," she said.

"That's the whole point," Denise assured her.

Now, as they hurried up the hall, Denise asked, "When's Nora coming back?"

"I thought she'd be here this morning," Jennifer told her.

Jason was the first to see the girls coming toward them. There was no telling what Mitch and Tommy would do when they saw them. And he couldn't face Jennifer — not yet, not until he got used to the idea that she liked him. He dropped back and darted up another corridor.

Tommy and Mitch stopped dead in their tracks.

"What'll we do?" Mitch asked.

"Act normal," Tommy said. He whipped out a comb and ran it through his sandy brown hair.

Mitch squared his shoulders and moved his arms away from his body.

As Jennifer and Denise approached, Tommy smiled his here-I-am-girls smile. Mitch said, "Hiya."

Denise said, "Nora really must have been" — the girls separated to pass them — "bitten" — the boys turned to stare after them — "by the bug."

"Hear that?" Tommy said. " 'Smitten'."

"Smitten?" Mitch said.

"Yeah. It's an old-fashioned word; it means — " Tommy broke off. He wasn't certain what it meant, but he was sure it had something to do with being in love. "Denise was talking about Jennifer's crush on Jason!"

"I thought she said 'bitten.' "

"I'm telling you, Pauley, Jennifer's in love."

"Yeah, but with Jason?"

Though he didn't admit it, Tommy was having the same trouble believing it. Why would Jennifer have anything to do with Jason Anthony when he, Tommy Ryder, was in the class? He suspected she really liked *him* and was playing hard to get.

Usually, Jennifer loved French class. Today, she had a hard time keeping her mind on the verb conjugation.

When Mr. Armand called her name, she was startled back to reality. "Try the next verb," he said.

"Love," someone prompted her.

Love, she thought, finding her place in the book. The word jumped out at her. LOVE! Her palms felt clammy and her mouth was suddenly dry. She couldn't conjugate that!

"Are you ready, Jennifer?" Mr. Armand prompted.

Jennifer gulped. "To love," she began. She adjusted her book. "I love — "

There were a few snickers behind her. Tommy leaned across the aisle and jabbed Jason.

Jennifer clear her throat. "You love; he loves."

"Very good, Jennifer," Mr. Armand said. "But we'd prefer it in French."

"I am so humiliated," Jennifer said at lunch. "Here it is a French class, and I'm conjugating in English!"

"It's easy to slip in and out of languages, when you think in them," Denise said. Because she'd spent so much time in Swiss schools, she spoke French fluently and often slipped into it without realizing it.

"Jen wasn't thinking in any language," Susan Hillard said.

"I sure wouldn't want to decline *love*," Tracy said coyly.

Amy Williams laughed. "You decline *sentences*, Tracy; you *conjugate* verbs."

Tracy said, "I was making a *joke*."

"She's got a point." Lucy Armanson picked up on the double meaning of the word decline. "No one wants to turn love down."

Jennifer phoned Nora from the pay phone in the front hall.

"Why aren't you here?" she asked.

"I felt rotten again this morning."

"Are you coming tomorrow?"

"I hope so. What's been happening?"

"For openers I made a complete idiot out of myself in French."

"How?"

"I haven't time to tell you now. I'll stop over after school, okay?"

"Terrific. Oh, Jen? Will you bring my scarf?"

Jennifer caught up with Mr. Mario outside homeroom. Behind her, Jason pretended to study a bulletin board.

"I don't have the scarf," Mr. Mario told her. "When no one claimed it, I turned it in to lost and found."

Jennifer couldn't get to the lost and found room, a closet in the administration offices, until after the last bell; by that time the scarf had disappeared.

She went out the side door where she'd told Denise she'd meet her. It had turned colder, the springlike air replaced by the smell and feel of late fall.

She pulled her sweater close around her as she watched Jason weaving his skateboard between cars in the parking lot. He had something on his head. From this distance it looked like a Mickey Mouse hat — except for the colors.

When he saw Jennifer, he glided over. He was wearing —

"Nora's scarf!" Jennifer exclaimed.

Susan and Amy waltzed down the stairs.

"You growing rabbit ears?" Susan said to Jason.

"Right," Jason said. "So I can get all the channels."

"You have to be plugged in first," Susan said.

They laughed as they headed toward Amy's mother's waiting car.

Jason tagged after them on his board. "Very funny, Hillard," he said. "A knee-slapper if I ever heard one."

Taking advantage of the distraction, Jennifer marched down the stairs after him. She was about to snatch the scarf off his head when he veered left and vanished around the side of the building.

"You bring that scarf back here, you creep!" Jennifer shouted. She decided to circle the building from the other direction. Perhaps she could catch him that way.

She was at the corner ready to make the turn when she heard a voice behind her. "Is this what you're looking for?"

She spun around and looked directly into Tony's dark, shining eyes.

He looped the scarf over her neck and stood there holding both ends. "You sure are a fighter."

"It's Nora's scarf," she said as though that explained everything.

He studied her thoughtfully. "You look different," he said.

It was the makeup. Maybe no one had said anything because she looked so ridiculous they were afraid of hurting her feelings. They were probably all laughing at her right this minute. "How?" she asked.

He shook his head. "I'm not sure." He stepped back and cocked his head. "Maybe it's your new pin." He put his forefinger under the black button on her sweater collar. " 'Extinct is forever.' That's food for thought."

She smiled. "It's not new. I just haven't worn it in a while."

Denise materialized, saying, "Did you pass. . . ?" Her voice trailed off when she saw the look in Jennifer's eyes.

Feeling the heat of Denise's inquiring gaze, Jennifer said, "Tony rescued Nora's scarf."

Tony reached into his brown leather bomber's jacket pocket. "Did I pass, you ask," He dangled a set of car keys from his index finger. "Need I say more?"

Denise reached up and gave him a hug. "Now you can teach me!"

"Congratulations," Jennifer said as she backed away. "See you, Denise."

"Don't you want a ride?" Tony asked.

Jennifer hesitated. Was he only asking to be polite? she wondered. And there was something else, something niggling at the periphery of her mind.

"Sure, Jen, come on," Denise said.

"You're safe, I promise," Tony said.

"Oh, it's not that." She was quick to assure him.

"Then come on."

"All right, I will," she said. Whatever it was she was forgetting couldn't be so important it couldn't wait.

Denise and Tony started for the car chattering excitedly. Jennifer took up the rear.

"Hey, Jen!" Steve Crowley called from the top of the steps.

Jennifer waved.

"Wait a minute!"

Tony looked back. "It's the BMW," he said.

Jennifer nodded. "I'll be right there."

Steve joined her on the sidewalk. "Got a minute?"

"Not now," Jennifer said, as she stepped off the curb.

"But I have to talk to you about the hayride."

"Call me later, okay? I don't want to keep Denise waiting." She turned and ran to catch up with Tony.

At the dining room window, Denise watched as Jennifer climbed into the front seat. Tony had had the nerve to drop his own sister off first. "This is getting ridiculous!" she said aloud.

Jennifer was plainly in love with her brother. Everytime she looked at him it was with adoration. And Tony was eating it up. Jennifer was setting herself up for real heartbreak.

She remembered wishing Tony had gotten involved with someone like Jennifer instead of Jessica. "Someone *like* Jennifer," she repeated now. "Not Jennifer!"

She sighed and let the lace curtain fall back over the window.

"Want me to close the window?" Tony asked Jennifer as he pulled away from the curb.

"It's okay," Jennifer said.

"You look cold huddled in the corner like that."

She did feel cold, but she suspected it was nerves more than the actual temperature. "I'm fine, really."

"This is my favorite time of year," Tony said.

"It's been really nice the last week," Jennifer said. "But today!"

"Cold, crisp air with a clear sky and a shining sun," Tony said. "What more could a person ask?"

"Warm air and trees full of green leaves — or at least buds."

"The trees are beautiful now." He pulled up beside Greatneck Park. "Come on, I'll show you."

Jennifer was out of the car before he got to her door.

"Don't be so quick," he said. "A man likes to open a door for a woman."

Woman! The word reverberated in her head.

Tony directed her attention to the tree-tops as they ambled along the stone path.

"It's not peak time," he said. "Not until all the leaves are gone, but you can get an idea." He pointed to a towering elm that had lost most of its leaves.

The delicate tracery of bare branches silhouetted against the milky-blue sky was breathtaking. "It's beautiful!"

"I told you," Tony said.

With her head thrown back, Jennifer spun to look at other trees, other designs. "They're all beautiful!"

Tony laughed. "Careful. You'll get dizzy."

She already was! She slowed to a stop. "How come I've never seen that before?"

"You've seen it," Tony said. "You just haven't paid attention."

They turned east and Jennifer was suddenly aware of two dark shapes stretching out from their feet on a slight diagonal. Their shadows! Each was long and lean and, even with the space between them, they looked good together.

Jennifer was so absorbed in her discovery she stumbled over a tree root. Tony reached to steady her but she had already recovered.

"You'd better hold on to me," he said. "I wouldn't want you to fall."

After a moment's hesitation, Jennifer grabbed hold of the knit waistband on the back of his jacket.

"Hold on to *me*, Jen," he said as he reached back to take her hand. "Not my jacket."

Chapter 11

At eight-thirty when Nora called, Jennifer remembered what she'd forgotten. And Nora was not about to let her forget it again.

"I thought you were coming over after school," Nora said.

"Oh, Nora, I'm sorry," Jennifer apologized. "I . . . forgot." As bad as that sounded, Jennifer knew the truth was best. "Denise and I — "

Nora hung up.

Jennifer couldn't believe she'd done that. She looked at the receiver, shook it, and returned it to her ear. Dial tone. She hung up. Nora had a right to be angry, but this was ridiculous. They'd always been able to talk through their differences before. She'd call her back. Maybe if she told Nora about Tony — She hadn't wanted to do that over the phone, but there didn't seem to be any other choice. If she knew what Jennifer'd been going through.

The phone rang. Thank heaven! Nora'd come to her senses.

Jennifer picked it up. "Hi, I was just going to call you."

"I should've saved my quarter," Steve Crowley said.

Jennifer was flustered. "Oh, Steve, hi! I thought it was Nora. I promised to go over there after school, and I, uh, forgot."

"Yeah, well, you looked pretty busy." There was an edge to his voice.

"Tony Hendrix got his driver's license today," she said. "And he wanted to drive Denise and me home. I had a lot of homework and stuff so. . . ." her voice trailed off. She suspected Steve wasn't buying any of it.

"Oh," Steve said, and then he didn't say anything.

Finally, Jennifer said, "You wanted to talk to me about something?"

"The hayride," he said. "I've been thinking Joan's probably right. Chili might not be a good idea. I could borrow warmers and dishes from my father, but we'd have all that cleaning up to do."

"And everybody doesn't like chili," Jennifer put in.

"Everybody doesn't like hot dogs, either."

The kitchen doorbell rang.

"Can I call you back, Steve? Someone's at the door." Without waiting for an answer, Jennifer hung up.

She looked through the window in the door. No one was there. She opened the door and peeked out. "Who's out there?" Jennifer said into the darkness.

A voice answered, " 'I'm nobody; who are you?' "

"Jason," Jennifer said wearily.

Jason's head popped out from behind a bush. His red hair was illuminated by the light from the window. "You're Jason?" he said. " 'Then there's a pair of us. Don't tell.' "

"Come on, Jason. Emily Dickinson isn't your style."

"I don't know." He stepped around the bush to the door. "There's a bit of the poet in all of us."

Jennifer sighed. It was getting late and she still had to talk to Nora and finish her homework. "What do you want, Jason?"

"What a person wants and what he gets — "

"Jason, will you please cut it out. I don't have all night."

" 'So little time,' " he quoted from her T-shirt.

"Jason!"

"You're beautiful when you're angry."

She turned on her heel and started back into the house.

"Will you go to the hayride with me?" Jason blurted.

Her hand poised to slam the door behind her, Jennifer stopped cold. "What?"

"I mean, if you're going — " His voice cracked.

She turned to face him.

"You probably . . . uh . . . don't want to — go with me, I mean. I'd understand if you didn't, but I figured, well, if we're both going. . . ." He shrugged.

"Gee, Jason, I don't know." The thought of going with someone had never occurred to her. She and Nora had decided after the Halloween dance, when they both asked Steve and ended up with nobody, that they preferred going on their own. And now Jason, of all people, was asking her to the hayride! It was just too much.

Jason backed away. "Listen, Jen, forget I asked, okay?" He disappeared into the shadows. In a few seconds, she heard the skateboard clacking down the drive. It sounded so forlorn.

"Jason? Wait!"

The telephone rang. Nora!

"I'll talk to you tomorrow," she called after him.

Grabbing the phone on the fourth ring,

she said, "Finally! I thought you'd never call."

"If I knew you felt like that, I'd've called a lot sooner."

Jennifer recognized Tommy Ryder's voice, but she couldn't believe her ears. "Who is this?" she asked.

"You know who it is, Jen," Tommy said. "You don't have to cover up. I like girls who express their feelings."

If he wasn't careful, she would. "What do you want, Tommy?" she said between clenched teeth.

"I thought I'd give you a thrill, take you to the hayride."

"Don't do me any favors!" Jennifer said and slammed down the phone.

As soon as she'd calmed down, she dialed Nora.

The line was busy.

Perched on the edge of the coffee table facing her brother, Denise said, "Jennifer is very special."

Tony boosted himself to his elbow. "You won't get an argument from me on that."

"That's what I'm afraid of," Denise said.

Tony looked at her quizzically.

"She likes you, Tony."

Tony smiled. "And I like her."

Denise groaned and rolled her eyes. This was more difficult than she'd anticipated.

"So what's the problem?" Tony asked her.

"She doesn't just like you; she *really* likes you."

He still didn't seem to understand. "What's so bad about that? Friends should 'really' like one another."

Denise shot to her feet. "Tony, listen to me. Jennifer Mann is in love with you!"

Tony blinked twice. Then, he swung his feet off the den couch to the ivory carpet. "Come on, Denise," he said.

"I'm telling you the truth."

"She's only fourteen," he said.

"Thirteen," Denise said. "You forget, I'm a year older than everyone else in the class."

"All the more reason," he said.

"Reason for what?" Denise demanded.

"Look, Denise, Jen is a nice girl. I like her. But not as a *girl* friend. She knows that. And she feels the same about me."

"Are you sure?"

The telephone rang. Denise looked at it resentfully. Picking it up, she snapped, "Hello."

Tony left the room. Denise'd have to continue her conversation with him later.

"Is something wrong?" Nora asked.

"Oh, Nora. Hi. Nothing's wrong," Denise said.

Despite her words, Denise sounded as though she felt Nora were intruding.

"You coming back to school tomorrow?" Denise continued. "Everybody misses you."

I'll bet, Nora thought. "I'm feeling terrific." Getting to the point of her call, she added, "Denise, did you see Jennifer today?"

"Why?" Denise asked warily. Jennifer and Nora were best friends. Just how much had Jennifer told her?

"Oh, no reason. I was just wondering."

"Didn't you talk to her?"

"Oh, sure. Just a little while ago. But she sounded a little strange," Nora said. "And I thought since the two of you've been spending so much time together —"

"That's a joke," Denise interrupted.

Nora was confused. "Didn't you do something after school today?"

"Is that what she told you?"

Nora hadn't given Jennifer much chance to tell her anything. "She was supposed to stop over and she didn't. When I asked her about it, she *did* mention your name."

Nora didn't know about Tony! This was far worse than Denise had imagined. "Nora," she said. "we've got a problem."

"Problem?" Nora asked.

"Jennifer's in love with Tony! I can't believe she didn't tell you."

Nora was stunned. "Tony? How does Tony feel?" Nora asked.

"He thinks she's a nice *kid*." Denise emphasized the last word meaningfully. "And he doesn't believe Jen thinks of him as anything but a friend. I'm afraid she's going to get hurt."

"We have to do something!" Nora said. "Distract her somehow. But how?"

"You know her better than I do," Denise said. "You should be able to come up with something."

Nora mulled that over. What would interest Jennifer enough to make her forget about Tony? Only one thing: "A project!" she said. "Jennifer never turns down a chance to help the needy."

Denise's instant enthusiasm was dampened by a practical thought. "But what? She's already saving every endangered animal left alive."

"It'd have to be something important," Nora said. "A person maybe. Someone she knows. Someone who really needs help."

They fell silent, thinking.

Finally, Nora, half joking, said, "Someone like Jason Anthony."

Chapter 12

"Jason Anthony is perfect!" Nora exclaimed the next morning.

"I agree," Denise said.

The two of them had come to the lounge of the girls' room where they could talk.

"I thought about him all last night," Nora said. "There's no one better."

"Pure genius," Denise said of Nora's project idea.

Someone came in, cutting off their dialogue.

"There's no one needier," Denise whispered.

Nora snickered.

"Shhh!" Denise warned her. "It'll never work if we let anyone know."

Nora clamped her hand over her mouth.

The door swung open. Jennifer rushed in. Taking in the scene, she thought, Nora's sick again! "I'll get someone!" she said as she backed out.

Abruptly, Nora stopped laughing. "For what?" she asked.

Jennifer took a tentative step forward. "You're not sick?"

"I'm fine."

"That's a relief!" Jennifer said. She stepped aside to let the door close behind her. "When I saw you two rush inside, I was sure there was something wrong. I mean: Before the bell? No one comes inside then."

"Only when it's necessary," Denise said.

She and Nora exchanged conspiratorial glances.

Jennifer didn't notice. "Nora?" she began. She would've preferred to talk to her friend alone, but she didn't want to let the rift between them get any wider. "I'm really sorry about yesterday."

Nora tossed her curly head. "Forget it," she said earnestly. "I have."

Jennifer wasn't convinced. It was too easy. She opened her mouth to speak.

The bell rang.

Andy Warwick came down the hall shaking his head. He'd come early this morning to take a history makeup test. Mr. Robards had put him in the rock room. The large, shelf-lined storage space filled with rock and fossil specimens was adjacent to the lounge of the girls' room.

He hailed Tommy Ryder and Mitch Pauley, who dodged their way across the hall to his side.

"What's up?" Mitch asked.

"Jason's perfect," Andy said in a daze.

Andy adjusted his black leather dog collar. "I heard them say so. I was in the rock room — "

Tommy and Mitch nodded knowingly. They'd done their turns in the rock room.

"Who was it?" Mitch asked.

Just then, Denise, Nora, and Jennifer emerged from the girls' room.

Tommy's jaw dropped. "Those three?"

"Must've been," Andy said, shaking his head incredulously. " 'No one better,' " Andy quoted.

"They said *that*?" The more he knew, the harder it was for Tommy to accept. He had asked Jennifer to the hayride to give her a chance to come to her senses. It was beginning to look as though nothing could save her.

" 'Pure genius,' " Andy said.

"Jason Anthony?" Mitch said.

"What else'd they say?" Tommy asked.

Andy shrugged. "Mr. Robards came in to get my test."

At lunch Tracy said, "Jen! You have makeup on! I can't even tell."

Amused, Jennifer asked, "Then what makes you think I've got any on?" She'd spent so much time twisting her long ponytail into a chignon and curling the wisps she'd pulled around her face, she hadn't had time to apply makeup.

"Because you look different," Tracy told her. "I've been trying to figure out for days why and now I know."

"You don't know a thing," Susan said. "It's her hair."

Tracy sat back to study Jennifer. "It's your hair!" she said at last.

"I'd love to wear mine like that but it's so much trouble," Lucy said.

"Yours is still too short," Nora said as she patted the top of Lucy's Afro.

"I like your hair the way you usually wear it," Amy said. "The more natural the better."

"Oh, I don't know," Jennifer said. "I think I look older this way."

Denise nudged Nora under the table.

Mia appeared and dropped into a chair. She held up her wrist to show off the bracelet she'd made with safety pins and black and white beads. "Whatd' you think?" she asked.

Jennifer was relieved. It took the focus off her.

"I saw one just like it at the mall for thirty dollars," Mia went on.

"How much did yours cost?" Lucy asked her.

"I had the safety pins," Mia said, "and my mom had the elastic thread. The beads were about five dollars."

"You could go into business," Nora said.

"I was thinking about that. I could make two a week — three if I skipped homework — charge six, seven dollars — "

"Too much!" Tracy said, her eyes fixed on a distant point.

"I'll bet I could get ten easy," Mia defended.

"Too much!" Tracy said again.

Mia shot to her feet. "What do you know?" She stalked off.

Tracy tore her glance away from Steve Crowley and Brad Hartley, who were standing in the cafeteria line. The two best-looking boys in the class standing side by side! It was too much. "Where's Mia going?" she asked. "I wanted to order a bracelet."

Everyone laughed.

A fly hovered over the pudding section. Jason reached over the brass rail and closed his hand around it. Easy. Flies that survived this late in the season were slow. Now that he had it, what could he do with it? He looked around the room.

It buzzed in his hand as he approached the girls' table.

"Here comes trouble," Amy said under her breath.

Jennifer turned. She was glad to see the mischievous look in Jason's eye. It was so different from the embarrassed one she'd seen there last night. It made her smile.

At a nearby table, Mitch's jaw dropped. "You might be right," he said to Tommy. "She's actually smiling at him!"

Jason's glance swept over the girls' table, coming to rest on Nora's prune whip. Perfect, he thought. It's even the right color. Having selected the target, he cast his eyes upward. "Did you see that hole up there?" When the girls tipped back their heads to look at the ceiling, he dropped the fly and darted away.

"What was that all about?" Nora dug into her dessert without looking and lifted a spoonful to her mouth.

Something flew off her spoon.

"It's alive!" Lucy shrieked.

Nora dropped her spoon.

Her eyes still on the ceiling, Tracy said, "Where? What? I don't even see a hole."

"Try looking at Jason's head," Susan said.

Jennifer waited by the side door while Nora checked with her teachers about makeup work. She scanned the parking lot for Tony.

When she saw Jessica Hartnett, in a white fake-fur jacket and slim black skirt, round the corner with a boy, her heart lurched, regaining its balance only when she realized it wasn't Tony. They passed on the sidewalk below her and paused beside a red convertible parked in the closest row, giving Jennifer the chance to scrutinize Jessica unnoticed.

She used her hands when she talked, her incredibly long nails slicing the air dramatically. And she blinked a lot — a result, Jennifer decided, of the weight of her heavy mascara.

She smiled up at her escort as he held the door for her.

"A man likes to hold a door for a woman," Tony said in Jennifer's head. Jessica was the kind of girl who was born knowing that, Jennifer thought.

She fluttered her eyelids the way Jessica did. The resulting strobe effect made the convertible appear to stop and start as it peeled out of the parking lot.

"Got something in your eye?" Steve Crowley said at her elbow.

Her eyes flew open wide. She'd promised to call him back last night. She wouldn't mention it; he'd probably forgotten.

"Steve! Hi!" she said, trying not to blink at all.

"Thought you were going to call me back last night," he said.

"I was?" She flushed under his steady gaze. Honesty meant too much to her for her to be a convincing liar. "Oh, right. I did say that. Listen, I'm sorry. Things kinda got out of hand last night."

"What things?" he asked.

Jennifer laughed uncomfortably. "You know. Things."

"No, Jen, I don't know."

Why did he have to be so direct? "Well," she began, doing some fast editing in her mind. "First Jason stopped over, and then I had to finish my homework and call Nora."

Steve's mind stuck on the word Jason and he couldn't get beyond it. He'd overheard Tommy saying something about Jen having a thing for Jason. Tony Hendrix was one thing, but *Jason*?

Nora plowed through the door balancing a leaning tower of books. "I'll never catch up!" she said breathlessly.

Jennifer moved to help her.

"Let me help," Steve offered.

"We can manage," Nora said. "Thanks anyway."

When they were out of earshot, Nora

asked, "What's with Steve? He looks strange."

"I thought so, too," Jennifer said.

"Finally!" Nora said when they were settled in her room. "A chance to talk!"

"I've got so much to tell you, I don't know where to begin," Jennifer said.

"I do!" Nora said. "Jason!"

"Jason?" Jennifer felt a pang of disappointment. At the same time, she was relieved that she could keep her feelings for Tony all to herself for a little while longer. "You want to talk about Jason?"

"Something has to be done about him," Nora said launching directly into her and Denise's plan. "He's getting creepier by the minute."

"He asked me to the hayride," Jennifer said.

Nora's jaw dropped. "When?"

"Last night."

"You were walking around with that bit of information all day and you didn't tell me?"

"I tried calling you last night; the line was busy. Even if I could've gotten through, you were so mad at me."

"Oh, that," Nora said. "Forget it. I was feeling sorry for myself — being sick and all." She hoped this small part of the truth would satisfy Jennifer. It wouldn't do either of them any good if she told Jen the rest: that she'd been jealous of Denise until she'd found out about Tony. She didn't plan to mention Tony at all. The less said the better — at least until Jennifer was involved in The Project. "What'd you tell Jason?"

"Nothing, really. It was all so strange. He asked me, and before I had a chance to say anything, he took it all back," Jennifer explained. "He has such a poor self-image."

Saying, "Strike *self*, and change *poor* to rotten," Nora watched Jennifer for her reaction.

"I don't think he's all that bad," Jennifer said, taking the bait. "We contribute to it, you know."

Good old Jennifer, Nora thought, I knew I could count on you. "Come on, Jen. Jason Anthony is hopeless!"

"All he needs is someone to bring out his good qualities."

"If you can find them," Nora goaded.

"I don't think it'd be any harder than — " Searching for the right words, Jennifer broke off.

"Saving whales?" Nora offered.

Jennifer laughed. "You make him sound like a project or something."

"Why not? He needs help; you can help

him. I can see your new pin: Save Jason; He's the Only One of His Kind."

"Nora! I couldn't do that. Jason's a person."

"Does that make him less important than a whale?"

"Of course not, but — "

"Jen, think about it," Nora urged. "It's a chance to really help somebody and see the results."

"What would I do?"

"What do you do with your other projects?"

"First, I learn all I can about them, and then I decide what I can do that'll do the most good."

"You already know a lot about Jason, so you're half there."

One part of Jennifer was reluctant to consider the plan; another was already racing ahead trying to decide how she could best uncover the real Jason. "I suppose I could try," she said.

Dear Diary, I finally had the chance to talk to Nora. But a funny thing happened. I didn't mention Tony. Not a single word. I'm not sure why. I was dying to tell her everything, but when the time came, I just couldn't. Besides, we got sidetracked on Jason.

* * *

When the telephone rang, Jennifer put her diary on the nightstand. Eight-thirty. Nora was right on time — proof she was no longer angry. Jennifer pulled her pink comforter up around her as she picked up the phone.

"Have you got a plan?" Nora asked.

"Not yet," Jennifer answered. "If I don't think about it, maybe something'll come to me."

"Anything else new?"

"Not much since I saw you, but there's a whole lot I forgot to tell you."

"I'm all ears," Nora said.

Jennifer had Nora's scarf over her shoulders and she fingered it as she said, "I got your scarf. I forgot to bring it today." On purpose, she admitted to herself. The scarf reminded her of Tony; she wanted to keep it as long as she could.

Nora reached over to turn down the volume on Trilogy, her favorite group. "Bring it tomorrow," she said. "What else did you forget?"

"Tommy Ryder," Jennifer said.

Nora laughed. "That's easy to understand."

"Wait! You haven't heard it all," Jennifer said. "He asked me to the hayride!"

After a pause, Nora began to laugh uncontrollably.

"Nora!" Jennifer said, laughing herself. "Stop it!"

Nora laughed all the harder.

"How can you laugh at Tommy like that?" Jennifer teased. "He's the most popular boy in the class."

"So he thinks," Nora managed to say. She caught her breath. "Wait, now, I have something else to — " Laughter cut her off. She tried again. "I'm not even going to ask what you said to him!" Finally, she was in control. "The amazing part is you're still here. Not one, but two, boys asked you out and you're — "

"Still here?" Jennifer interrupted.

"Remember when I went out with Brad, you said you'd die if someone asked you out?" Nora explained.

"I never expected it'd be Jason and Tommy!" Jennifer said.

That set Nora off again.

When she and Nora had finished their conversation, Jennifer added a postscript to her diary entry: *What would I do if Tony asked me out?*

Then, she got out her nail file.

Chapter 13

Most of their group was huddled with Mia, placing orders for bracelets, when Jennifer arrived at school. It gave her the chance to talk to Denise and Nora privately.

"I don't think I can do it," she said. Although she'd lain awake thinking about Jason, she hadn't come up with a single plan.

"If you can't," Nora said, "no one can."

"We'll help," Denise put in.

"But what do I do? I can't just go up to him and say, 'You're a creep, Jason and — ' "

Nora snickered. "Why not? Everybody else does."

"Be serious, Nora," Jennifer reprimanded.

"The best thing you can do is talk to him, Jen," Denise said. "He'll listen to you."

"Yeah, but — "

"There he is!" Nora exclaimed as Jason cruised around the corner on his board. "I'll get him!"

"Wait! Nora!" Jennifer said. Too late. Nora was already racing down the steps. "I can't talk to him *here*," she said helplessly.

Denise agreed. "There isn't time. Why don't you meet him after school?"

At the foot of the stairs, Nora pointed to Jennifer. Jason had one foot on the skateboard, his arms crossed over his chest. He squinted up at Jennifer.

Jennifer flushed. This was ridiculous. She waved self-consciously.

"You want to see me?" he called up to her.

The whole class would hear. She started down the stairs. Jason started up. They met halfway.

"I thought maybe if you had some time after school we could talk," Jennifer said in hushed tones.

Jason looked at her suspiciously. "About what?"

About your manners, Jennifer thought. "About — " She searched her mind for a legitimate subject. " — the hayride!" Perfect. She'd never given him an answer to his invitation.

"What about it?" Jason asked.

The bell rang.

"Not now, Jason. After school, okay?" Jennifer turned and ran up the steps.

Jason plodded after her. At the door, he met up with Mitch and Tommy.

"What was all that about?" Tommy asked.

Jason shrugged. "She wants to talk to me."

"About what?" Mitch asked.

"The hayride."

Tommy nodded, then wondered, "Why would she want to talk to you about that?"

Shrugging, Jason opened his locker.

"You're not on the same committee," Tommy persisted.

Jason stashed his skateboard inside and took out his books. "I asked her," he said and then sprinted toward homeroom.

"You? Asked *her*?" Tommy repeated. He staggered backward, then drifted off, mumbling to himself.

Andy Warwick called out to him, but Tommy was in too much of a daze to hear him.

"What's with Ryder?" Andy asked Mitch.

"Jason asked Jennifer."

"Asked her what?"

Mitch slammed his locker door. "Beats me."

During lunch period, Steve came up to

the girls' table. "There's a meeting after school," he told Nora and Jennifer.

Jennifer looked at Nora. What would she do about Jason now?

"Jen can't make it," Nora told Steve.

"Why not?" Steve asked Jennifer.

"Jen has something very important to do," Denise answered for her.

Steve never took his eyes off Jennifer. "More important than the food committee meeting?"

"Well," Jennifer began. "Maybe I could — "

"Much more," Nora interrupted. "But don't worry, Steve, I'll be there. I'll take notes and pass them on to Jen."

Steve said, "I suppose if you can't make it, you can't make it."

Tracy sat dumbfounded through the entire conversation. She couldn't imagine anything keeping *her* away from a meeting with both Steve Crowley and Brad Hartley. When Steve was out of earshot, she asked Jennifer, "What're you doing after school?"

"Nothing important," Nora answered.

Jason was waiting outside when Jennifer came through the side door. It had been a long wait. She had purposely delayed her departure until most of her classmates were gone.

"Where're we having this talk?" he asked her.

Jennifer looked around. She hadn't thought about it before, but the campus was not the place — too many curious eyes. "Why don't we just walk?"

"Toward your house?"

"That'd be fine."

She started off. Jason hopped on his skateboard and followed along.

Across the parking lot, Tony leaned on the roof of the BMW watching them. He'd thought a lot about what Denise had told him. Jennifer'd helped him over some rough spots by listening sympathetically without offering unwanted advice. She was bright and interesting and she cared. He'd like to continue the friendship, but he didn't want to interfere with her relationships with her own classmates. Seeing her with a boy her own age relieved his mind. Obviously, Denise was wrong. Jennifer *did* understand their relationship. To be on the safe side, he'd phone her later to make it absolutely clear.

When they were a block away from the school, Jason shot ahead of Jennifer. Then he waited for her to catch up and pass him. He lagged behind for a while and then he scooted on ahead.

As they approached the Cedar Groves Pharmacy, he said, "I'm going to get some gum."

Jennifer followed him inside, wandering the aisles while he made his choice. A display of false fingernails caught her eye. She looked at her hands. She'd filed all her nails to the same length last night and applied red polish, about the shade of Jessica Hartnett's, but she'd removed it all. Her nails were just too short.

She craned her neck to see what Jason was up to. He was still poring over the candy rack. She took the fingernails to the girl at the cosmetic counter and dug out her wallet.

Outside, Jason mounted the skateboard sideways and glided along beside Jennifer. "Are we talking yet?"

"How can we talk when you're riding that thing?" Jennifer said. "You're either a block ahead of me or a block behind and it keeps clacking!"

Jason thought about that; then he dutifully stepped down off the board and put it under his arm. They walked along in silence. Finally, Jason said, "I feel like I'm walking The Last Mile."

Jennifer laughed. "That's funny, Jason. It really is. You have a good sense of humor." She paused. Then, she said, "Actually, you have many good qualities."

Jason blew a bubble.

"Jason?"

He crossed his eyes to watch it grow.

"Are you listening?"

It burst. As he peeled it off his face, he said, "For what? I know this lecture by heart."

Jennifer felt a pang inside. She deserved that. "I don't mean it as a lecture. I just want to help."

"Who says I need help?"

"Do you want people to call you a creep?"

"I don't mind." He smiled impishly. "As long as they're sincere."

"Be serious, Jason," Jennifer said. "That's part of your problem; no one can talk to you."

"Maybe that's their problem," he said. "Maybe they don't try hard enough."

Jennifer sighed. "I'm trying, Jason. As hard as I know how. You're not giving me a chance."

Jason thought about that. "Okay," he said at last. "Shoot."

"Well, like I said, you have all kinds of good qualities, but you hide them behind pranks and things."

"I'm good at pranks," Jason protested.

Jennifer laughed. "That's because you get so much practice."

"Like they say: Practice makes perfect."

"I wish you'd practice something else. Try something, for a week maybe, and see if it doesn't make a difference in how everyone treats you."

Jason was wary. "Like what?"

"Like not putting insects or your fingers in people's food for one thing."

He nodded thoughtfully. "Okay." He could manage to restrain from doing those things for a week. There were other tricks he could pull, and a week wasn't all that long.

"No pranks of any kind," Jennifer said as though she were plugged into his thoughts.

Jason dropped his skateboard and jumped on.

"And no skateboard!"

Now, she was asking too much. "For a whole week?"

"Will you do it, Jason?"

His shoulders drooped as he stepped off the board. "I guess so," he said reluctantly.

Jennifer beamed. "It'll make a big difference, Jason, you'll see."

Jason pushed the board ahead of them with his foot. "Why is it when people want to help you, they always tell you what you *shouldn't* do, never what you should?"

Jennifer didn't know the answer. "I guess people have to figure that part out for themselves," she said.

* * *

"How was the meeting?" Jennifer asked after dinner when she phoned Nora. "Did you accomplish anything?"

"Nothing. Brad wasn't there," Nora answered.

Jennifer laughed. "Nora! Be serious."

"Well, Steve and Joan fought it out. I listened. I think we decided on hot dogs and hamburgers."

"What do we have to do?"

"Nothing until Saturday. Steve's getting the food and Joan's taking care of the paper stuff. They'll need us to help cook and serve." Lying across her bed, Nora rolled to her stomach. "What happened with Jason?"

"He thought I was giving him a lecture," Jennifer said.

"You were."

"I didn't want him to know it." Jennifer took up her pen and doodled absently on the scratch pad on her desk.

"Did you get anywhere?"

"I don't know. We talked for a long time. He has a terrific sense of humor."

"Sure he does," Nora said ironically. "I nearly had a *taste* of it yesterday at lunch."

The memory of the fly in Nora's prune whip sent a chill up Jennifer's spine. She shivered. "He promised me he wouldn't do anything like that again, and he's giving up his skateboard for a week."

"Jennifer Mann, you are a genius!"

After Nora hung up, Jennifer glanced at the scratch pad. She had covered two pages with variations of the name *Jennifer Hendrix*.

The telephone rang. She picked it up, saying, "Mann's Menagerie."

"Jen?"

It was Tony! No one else said her name like that.

"I was thinking about you," he said, not quite knowing where to begin. "So I thought I'd give you a call."

Jennifer looked down at her doodling. *Jennifer Hendrix*. The two names fit together just as their shadows did. "I was thinking about you, too," she said.

"I've never . . . had a girl for a friend before," he said, "and I just wanted you to know you sure have been a good one."

Jennifer's heart raced. Surely, he felt as she did.

Chapter 14

"Come with me to the girls' room," Jennifer whispered to Nora.

"Wait till the bell rings," Nora said. "I want to see how Jason looks without his skateboard. I wonder if we'll recognize him."

Jennifer dug her hands deeper into her jacket pockets. "Please, Nora." She edged toward the door.

Responding to the urgency in her friend's voice, Nora followed her inside. "You're not getting what I had?"

Jennifer shook her head. "I'm not sick."

"You look really tired."

Jennifer *was* tired. What with her hair and her face, she'd lost an hour's sleep every morning all week. This morning, she'd lost even more! But that wasn't the problem.

She pushed the door open with her shoulder and hurried inside, saying, "I can't zip my jeans."

Nora chuckled. "You can't what?"

"Nora! It's not funny!"

Nora noticed that Jennifer's hands were still in her pockets. "Oh, Jen!" she said. "You hurt your hands. What happened? Let me see."

Reluctantly, Jennifer drew one hand from its hiding place and held it out limply, palm down.

Nora burst out laughing. "Where did you get those nails?!"

"At the pharmacy," Jennifer said. "It took forever to glue them on and get them painted. Then I struggled into these pants and by the time I realized I couldn't zip them, there was no time to change."

"You're lucky long sweaters are in," Nora said.

Jennifer thought her problems were over, until English class, when she discovered she couldn't hold her pen. The nails kept colliding with one another or stabbing her in the palm. When she finally figured out a way, she couldn't write.

Then, in gym, she was benched when Joan Wesley complained Jennifer had scratched her as they both went for a volley ball shot.

She'd heard one had to suffer for beauty's sake. By lunchtime, she was beginning to wonder if it was worth it.

Mia was the only one who liked the nails. "But they're pretty boring with plain polish," she said. She held out her own. They were painted black with an orange stripe down the middle of each and glittery stars at the tips.

"I'd never have the time to do that," Jennifer objected.

Lucy folded herself into a chair, saying "What's with Jason?"

The others followed her gaze. Dressed in his camouflage fatigues, Jason sat alone with a book open on the table in front of him.

"No skateboard; no pranks. Is he sick or what?"

"He's trying to change his image," Nora explained.

"To what?" Mia asked. "The Invisible Man?"

"Don't tell me it was Jason's idea," Susan Hillard said.

"It was Jennifer's," Nora said. "A kind of project."

"And we should help all we can," Denise added. "Isn't that right, Jen?"

Jennifer hadn't been listening. She was trying to figure out how to hold her sandwich without tearing it to shreds.

"We're talking about Jason," Nora said

when Jennifer looked up blankly. "How we can help him."

Jennifer's mind caught up. "If everyone just talked to him."

Mia turned in her chair to stare at Jason. "A creep like that needs a lot more than talk."

"Some new clothes for starters," Lucy said.

"His mind is what needs improving," Tracy said.

Susan laughed. "You're just the one to do it."

Amy Williams joined them. "Did you see Jason? He looks like he's lost his best friend."

"He has," Susan said. "His skateboard."

"Jen's redoing him," Nora said.

"Really?" Amy seemed pleased. "I'd sure like to help. Get him on an exercise program, build him up."

"He'd still be a creep," Susan said.

"We should stop calling him 'creep'!" Jennifer exclaimed.

Tracy's eyes widened. "What *should* we call him?"

When they'd all stopped laughing, Amy said, "Coach is keeping the boys after school to do laps. Wanna stay and heckle them?"

Jennifer was the only one who declined.

"There's a special meeting of Save the Whales at four," she said. "We're helping Greenpeace with a letter-writing campaign."

After school, Nora said, "I don't think those nails are good for you, Jen."

The others had gone directly to the athletic field, but she'd decided to walk Jennifer to the door.

"You might be right," Jennifer said. "If I don't get used to them pretty soon, I'll flunk everything."

"I mean physically," Nora clarified. "Some kind of fungus can grow under them."

"Don't worry; I'll probably stab myself to death before that happens."

They were laughing so hard they didn't notice Tony pull up to the curb below them. He leaned out the window and called, "Jen?"

Jennifer's face underwent a series of changes before settling into a smile. She turned toward him. "Tony!"

"Have you seen Denise?" he asked.

"She's staying after."

Tony looked disappointed.

"But I'm not," Jennifer said. "Can you give me a lift?"

"You've got a meeting," Nora said under her breath.

Tony hopped out of the car and ran around to open her door. "I was headed for the mall," he said. "Want to ride along?"

She smiled up at him. "Sure." Out of the corner of her eye, she saw Nora standing alone at the top of the stairs watching her. She looked down at her hands. Knowing she was talking to Nora, she said silently to herself, I wouldn't be any help at the meeting anyway; I can't write letters with these nails.

"Tony dropped me off," Jennifer explained later when Nora answered the door. "I had to talk to you!" She followed Nora upstairs to the bedroom, the words tumbling out almost faster than she could think them. She told Nora about the other times she'd seen Tony. "I've been wanting to tell you for days," she concluded, "but you never said anything about my note and then you got sick and I forgot about it and — "

"What note?" Nora asked as she closed her bedroom door.

" '*Guess who was at the library last night?*' " Jennifer quoted.

"I never got any note," Nora said.

Jennifer brushed that aside. "So much has happened since! He's so wonderful! I even dream about him! And our shadows match! We even walk and — breathe! —

in sync." She began digging in her bag. "Wait'll you see what he bought me. We went to the mall for some tapes he wanted." She pulled out her SO MUCH TO DO . . . T-shirt, saying, "I was going to wear this today, but then I couldn't get my jeans zipped, and I wore the sweater 'cause it's longer, so I stuffed the T-shirt in here to wear to the meeting." She tossed it on Nora's bed.

"But you didn't get to the meeting?" Nora said.

"I didn't *have* to be there," Jennifer said. "It's voluntary." She peered into her bag. "Here it is!" She drew out a small package from which she unwrapped the tissue to reveal a small pewter whale. "Isn't it beautiful?" Without waiting for Nora's reaction, she continued, "We had the absolute best time! And I'm going with him again to help shop for Denise's birthday. We didn't have time today. Did you know her birthday is next week? I can't believe she never said a thing about it."

When Jennifer took a breath, Nora asked, "What do you talk about?"

Jessica Hartnett was the first thing that popped into Jennifer's head, but she didn't say it. After all, their conversation was no longer exclusively centered on Jessica. They talked about other things, too. "Nothing. Everything!" she said. "Today he asked me why I thought Sally sold seashells at the seashore."

Nora looked at her blankly.

"You can get shells for nothing there," Jennifer explained.

Nora was incredulous. "You talked about . . . tongue twisters?"

"We weren't talking about tongue twisters; we were talking about seeing things from another perspective."

"If you ask me," Nora said pointedly, "you don't have any perspective at all."

Jennifer rewrapped the pewter whale and returned it to her bag. "That's not fair, Nora," she said.

"It's true. You're so gone over Tony, you — "

"I'm not gone," Jennifer objected. "I just like him that's all. We're friends."

Nora lowered herself to the edge of the bed. "Steve Crowley is a friend. I don't see you following him around."

"So, I . . . like Tony. What's so bad about that?"

"You're going to get hurt, Jen."

"That's crazy. Tony's not like that."

"I don't mean he'd do it on purpose, but you're so wrapped up in him."

"What about you and Brad?" Jennifer interrupted.

"That's a whole different thing. We're the same age! And I like him, sure, but it's not making a zombie out of me."

Nora's words stung like a slap. "I've got to get home," Jen said. "I'll talk to you later." She was out of the room and down the stairs before Nora noticed she'd left her T-shirt behind.

Nora's not even trying to understand, Jennifer thought as she walked home. It made her sad to think about it. They'd been friends for so long, weathered so much, and now Nora seemed determined to spoil everything. I just won't talk about Tony at all, Jennifer decided.

As she dialed Jennifer, Nora reconfirmed her decision not to mention Tony. No matter what I say, she'll never understand, she thought.

As usual, they discussed what they would wear the following day. That settled, Jennifer said, "You didn't tell me what happened after school."

"A bunch of us went to Temptations when the boys finished running laps. Everybody's really excited about the Jason thing. They're all thinking up ways to help. Oh, and I had a long talk with Steve."

"What about?"

"You mostly. He says you never talk to him anymore. You're always too busy." Realizing that was an indirect reference to Tony, Nora paused. "But you know

Steve," she added, trying to minimize the remark.

"Right," Jennifer said. "If we don't tell him our innermost secrets. . . ." Her voice trailed off. If she wasn't careful, Nora would make a remark about Tony.

Dear Diary, Today was a yay/boo day. Tony and I went shopping at the Twin Rivers Mall. (Yay!) I missed a Save the Whales meeting. (Boo!) Tony asked me to help him pick out Denise's birthday present. (YAY!!) Nora's mad at me. (BOO!) I'm wondering: Will I ever be able to talk to her again without thinking about every word first?

She reread her entry. It looked as though it had been written by a first-grader.

I'm also wondering: she added, *Am I ever going to get used to these fingernails?*

P.S. I have a confession to make: I didn't tell you when Tony wants me to shop with him. Don't feel bad, I didn't tell Nora, either. But I have to tell somebody because it may be the biggest YAY/BOO of all. He wants me to go with him on Saturday — the day of the class hayride!!! What should I do?

Chapter 15

Lucy Armanson carried a garment bag over her arm as she ascended the school stairs. "Have you seen Jason?" she asked Jennifer and Nora.

Jennifer wouldn't have noticed him this morning even if she had seen him. She was disturbed about the tension between her and Nora which was obvious despite Nora's attempts to act as if nothing had happened.

Nora shook her head. "No. Why?"

Amy Williams came up the stairs struggling with a duffel bag. "Where's Jason?"

"Haven't seen him," Denise said.

An intent look on her pretty face, Tracy walked past them.

"Hey, space cadet," Susan Hillard called to her.

Tracy kept right on walking. "I'm looking for Jason," she said.

At her heels, Joan Wesley said, "So am I."

"Joan Wesley?" Nora said. "What is going on here?"

"He must be with Mia," Lucy decided, and then she skipped down the stairs.

Nora looked at Jennifer. "What would Jason be doing with Mia?"

Tommy Ryder sauntered over. "Why's everyone looking for Jason?" he asked.

Nora, Jennifer, and Denise shrugged.

Just then, Mia came around the corner. She was walking backwards, talking to someone out of view. She seemed to be coaxing whoever it was, urging him to follow her. Lucy ran over to join her.

A foot appeared. Then a leg. Finally, Jason Anthony bobbed into view.

Jennifer blinked in disbelief.

Susan Hillard guffawed.

Mitch Pauley dropped the basketball he was twirling.

Tommy Ryder put away his comb.

Nora's jaw dropped. "Will you look at that!"

Jason's hair was arranged in an explosion of fiery red spikes. A gold earring dangled from his left ear. His green eyes were boldly outlined in black. His freckled fingers poked through cut-off black leather driving gloves.

Mia took his hand and impatiently pulled him along after her. "What d'you think?" she called up to the others.

No one spoke.

Misinterpreting their silence for approval, Mia said, "It's not *that* good. Actually, we're not finished. I thought I'd dye his hair next — black. It should be very effective with his light skin, and we'll add some more earrings." She turned Jason's head to the side. His earring fell off.

Jennifer exhaled a breath of relief. At least Mia hadn't pierced his ear.

Lucy unzipped the garment bag. "Put this on, Jason." She dug out a tweed jacket and striped tie. "It's all I could find, but it's a start. I'll bring some more tomorrow."

"From punk to prep in one easy lesson," Susan scoffed.

The other girls crowded around Jason, making suggestions.

Nora exchanged confused glances with Denise. This was not what they had intended.

Tracy handed him an etiquette book. Amy thrust a set of barbells at him. Joan Wesley tucked a reading list in his pocket.

Jennifer was horrified. They're treating Jason as though he were a piece of clay, and it's all my fault! she thought.

After his initial confusion, Jason acted

as though he were the king of the prom, trying to make room on his dance program for everyone.

Between Jason The Project and preparations for the hayride, which was only a day away, the eighth grade was abuzz all morning. And no one could eat lunch.

Instead, they all watched Jason as he floated from table to table smiling and chatting like a politician at election time.

Tommy Ryder shook his head. "It must be catching," he said. "It's not just Jennifer; they've all gone crazy."

"Jason must have something," Mitch said.

"What?" Tommy asked. "He's creepier than ever. Except for that stupid jacket and that tie — whoever heard of a tie with a camouflage T-shirt? — he looks just like Andy."

"Yeah," Andy retorted, "and he's acting just like you, Ryder."

Tracy arrived at the girls' table brimming with excitement. "Guess who just asked me to the hayride," she said as she slid into a chair.

"Can't imagine," Susan said.

"Tommy Ryder!" Tracy exclaimed. "In the hall! Just before lunch! I told him it was late — the hayride's tomorrow — can you believe it? — but — "

"I didn't know we were going on dates,"

Lucy said. "Except for Mia, I mean."

Mia always went to class functions with Andy.

"I might surprise everybody tomorrow," Mia said, her eyes on Jason.

"And come alone?" Amy asked.

"No," Mia said. "With Jason."

"You can't," Tracy said. "Jennifer's going with Jason."

Everyone looked at Jennifer.

"Who says?" Jennifer asked.

"Tommy," Tracy said. "I didn't believe it at first, but then he showed me the note you wrote about meeting Jason at the library and — "

Jennifer shot to her feet and marched to Tommy's table with the other girls close at her heels.

"Tommy Ryder!" she challenged. "What makes you think I'm going to the hayride with Jason?"

Tommy scrambled to a safe retreat behind Mitch's chair. "He told me he asked you."

"Did he tell you I said 'yes'?"

"Not exactly." Tommy grinned sheepishly. Then a thought struck him. "Wait a minute. You're not going with Jason?"

"I am not," Jennifer said.

"Then why'd you turn me down?"

"You — you asked Jennifer?" Tracy sputtered.

"Don't blow a gasket, Tracy," Tommy told her. "I'm going with you."

"I wouldn't go with you if you were the last boy on earth," Tracy flung over her shoulder as she stormed off.

"Now look what you did, Jen," Tommy whined.

"What *I* did! You are the creep of creeps, Tommy Ryder!"

"Say, Jen," Mitch asked. "How about if you go with me?"

"Thank you, but no, thank you," Jennifer snapped. "I am not going to the hayride with Jason. I am not going with Tommy. And I am not going with you!"

Mitch's confusion was obvious. "Then who are you going with?"

"No one!" Jennifer said, adding, "I am not going to the hayride at all!" which surprised everyone, even herself.

Everyone chorused "You're not going to the hayride? Why?" except Nora and Denise, who thought they knew the answer.

It's hopeless, Nora wrote Denise later in study hall. *We'll never get Jen's mind off you-know-who. She's not thinking of anything or anyone but that person. She even left her* SO LITTLE TIME *T-shirt — the one I gave her — at my house yesterday, and she hasn't asked for it yet.*

There must be something we can do,
Denise wrote back.

What? Nora queried.

I could talk to her, Denise suggested.

Go ahead, but I don't think it'll do any good, Nora wrote.

"Are you two finished?" Susan hissed. "I'll never get my homework done if I have to sit here passing notes the whole period."

There was no chance to talk to Jennifer the rest of the day. When the last bell rang, Denise approached her.

Jennifer saw her coming. She wants to talk to me about Tony, she thought. It had been bad enough getting a lecture from Nora; there was no way Jennifer could sit still while Denise — his own sister — warned her about him. She hastily gathered her things and made for the door. "See you guys," she said. "I've got to get to the nursing home."

Once outside, Jennifer slowed her pace. She hoped Tony would come along. She needed to talk to him. She felt so cut off, so alone. It looked as if she and Nora would never be able to communicate openly again — not unless she stopped seeing Tony. And she just couldn't do that. Why did everything have to be so complicated?

Sitting on his skateboard, head resting on his hands, Jason was waiting for her when she returned from the nursing home.

"Hi," he said listlessly as she trudged up the driveway.

His hair had wilted.

"You look beat," Jennifer said.

He looked up at her. His eyes, with the smeared eyeliner, were like sad clown eyes. "You don't look so hot yourself."

Jennifer lowered herself to the stoop outside her back door. "Everybody's mad at me," she said.

He nodded sympathetically. "No one's mad at me."

"All they want to do is lecture me," she added.

"No one's lectured me," he said. "I haven't even heard the word *creep* in two days." He paused. "And I miss my skateboard at school." He sighed. "It's a great responsibility being popular."

She studied her long fingernails. The polish was beginning to chip. She picked at one. "I don't know why you let Mia do this to you."

He sighed. "It seemed like a good idea at the time."

"You're not going to let her dye your hair, are you?"

"I'm thinking about shaving it off," he said. "Or maybe trying a mohawk."

In spite of herself, Jennifer laughed. "Oh, Jason! You're not serious."

He shrugged. "How about Lucy's idea? Tweeds and ties?"

She felt a rush of sympathy. Here was a — a unique, interesting person turning himself into some generic nobody on the whim of other people. She tucked her hands under her and leaned toward him. "It's not you," she said gently. "None of it is you."

"What is?" Jason asked seriously.

Eric opened the door and leaned out. "Jeff says you should come in now," he told Jennifer. "Supper's ready."

Jennifer stood up. "You have to be yourself, Jason. Your best self." She had the vague sense that she was talking to herself as well as to Jason, and when he said, "I'm not always sure who that is," she had to admit she felt that way, too.

As she was about to go in, Jason scooted over to the stoop. "You dropped something," he said, reaching up to hand her a scarlet fingernail.

Inside, Jennifer tried removing the remaining nine. They wouldn't budge. Maybe she'd have to wait until they fell off one by one.

Seeing her distress, Jeff Crawford handed her an orange stick. "Pry them off with this."

Surprised, she asked. "What're you doing with an orange stick?"

"A trick I learned from Debby," he said. "They come in handy for all sorts of things: Scraping dirt from cracks; helping resident dragon ladies. . . ."

That, Jennifer knew, was a reference to her long nails. As she pried the first one loose, she asked, "How can a person tell if she's changing because she's growing up or because she isn't?"

"If she makes the change for herself," he said. "If it feels right for her — that'd tell her something."

"How do you know when it *feels* right?"

"When you don't have to ask," Jeff answered.

Jennifer scrubbed her face clean of makeup, undid her chignon, brushed her hair one hundred strokes, and still Nora hadn't called. Jennifer thought about calling her, but she had no idea what to say. The only thing Nora wanted to hear right now was that Jennifer had decided not to go shopping with Tony tomorrow.

She sat down at her desk and took out her diary. She stared at a blank page for a long time before she began to write.

Dear Diary, I'm going with Tony tomorrow. I didn't know that for sure until I heard myself say I wasn't going to the hayride. Maybe I did know. I just didn't want to admit it. I figured I could go with

Tony and not think about what I was missing. Maybe I could've if Tommy Ryder hadn't told everyone I was going with Jason. Then again, maybe I couldn't've. I like being with my friends. I like being with Tony, too. Why is life so full of hard choices?

She had another choice to make: What to wear tomorrow. It wouldn't be much fun without Nora to help her decide.

Chapter 16

"I didn't know about the hayride," Tony said to Denise.

Denise glared at him across the breakfast table. "Of course not. Jen didn't tell you. She didn't want you to know."

"Why would she do that?" Tony asked. "Jen's so straight-forward."

"*Usually*, you mean," Denise corrected him.

"But we're friends. Why would she keep something like that from me?"

Denise sighed. Sometimes her brother was as dense as a brick wall. "Because she's in love with you! I told you that. And that's not the only thing she's keeping from you. She missed a Save the Whales meeting to be with you," Denise informed him. "And she's wearing those stupid false fingernails because Jessica's are long and since you liked Jessica —"

"False fingernails?" Tony interrupted.

"You didn't even notice? Oh, Tony, do

you know anything about her at all?"

"I never notice things like that," Tony defended himself.

Denise felt a stab of remorse. She was being too hard on him. He might be older than she, but he knew far less about the subtleties of human relations. She reached over and touched his arm. "Maybe it's time you did."

Tony pushed his plate away. "What do you want me to do, Denise?"

"It's not what I want, Tony," she said softly. Then she slipped into her denim jacket. "I gotta go. I'm meeting some of the kids at school. We're going to ride out to the stables together." At the door, she turned to him. "I hope you do the right thing."

Tony sat motionless at the table for a long time after Denise had gone. Finally, he picked up the phone and dialed Jennifer.

When Jennifer heard his voice, her heart sank. He wasn't coming!

"Jen?" he said. "I — uh — thought I'd call. I got to thinking maybe you had something else to do today."

"Why?" she said. "Don't you want to go?"

"Oh, it isn't that," Tony assured her. "I just thought if you're busy, we could go another time."

"Today's fine," she said.

During the long pause that followed, Jennifer could feel her heart beating.

"Okay," Tony said at last. "I'll be there in a few minutes. I hope you're not dressed up," he added. "I'm in my grubbies."

She looked down at her burgundy Laura Ashley dress — a name she hadn't even heard of until she met Denise — and her patent leather shells with the suede inset — Jeff called them her Minnie Mouse shoes. "Are jeans okay?" she asked.

"Terrific," Tony said.

She dashed upstairs to change. To top her jeans, she chose a pink turtleneck and a white crew neck sweater. At the last minute, she grabbed Nora's scarf and tied it around her ponytail.

"Am I okay?" she asked when Tony arrived.

He smiled. With the ends of her silken pony tail over one shoulder and her face glowing with the natural blush of excitement, she looked especially good today. "You're more than okay."

They walked hand in hand to the car.

"Do you know that Denise didn't even tell anyone her birthday's next week?" she said as he pulled away from the curb. "I haven't come up with a single idea for a present. I hope you have some."

He glanced at her. "Do you mind if we

drive awhile before we go? I'd like to talk to you first."

Her heart skipped. What could he possibly have to say that couldn't wait? Obviously, she'd have to wait to find out. He had gone silent, his eyes straight ahead. She turned slightly sideways to look at him. Everything about him seemed quiet today, from the way his strong, square hands held the wheel to the look in his dark eyes. Brooding, she thought, remembering Heathcliff in *Wuthering Heights*.

Outside the Cedar Groves city limits, he turned his head briefly and smiled. "Jen?"

She faced forward. He was going to tell her he didn't want to see her again, and then he'd turn around and take her home.

He stopped at a red light. "Jen, you're really *something*," he said without looking at her.

She shifted uneasily. He was going to ask her to go steady!

"A couple of weeks ago, the world was a pretty bleak place to me," he continued. "And then you came along, and all that changed." He fell silent.

The rolling countryside was bathed in an autumn gold light, and here and there a gleaming silver silo blinked. Jennifer tried to concentrate on the scenery, but her breath felt ragged. No matter what he said, she was afraid she couldn't handle it.

"What I especially like about you, Jen," he said at last, "is your independence. You seem to know who you are and where you're going."

"I don't always feel that way," Jennifer said softly. "Most of the time, I'm not sure I'm going anywhere."

Tony laughed. "Oh, you *are* going places. Take my word for that." He reached over and took her hand. She felt the warmth of his touch pass through her like an electric current. "If somebody doesn't come along and spoil it all."

Puzzled, she asked, "Who would do that?"

He glanced at her and smiled. "Me?"

"That's ridiculous," she protested.

"I'm not so sure." He withdrew his hand and replaced it on the wheel. "The thing is, I don't think we've understood one another. I may have given you the wrong idea. I didn't mean to, but. . . ." When Jennifer didn't respond, he continued, "I think I'm in your way. I've been keeping you from all the things you usually do."

Sadness dropped inside her like a fog. She opened her mouth to protest, but he stopped her, saying, "It's true, Jen."

"I don't know what you mean," she said, her voice small.

"I think you do." As he put on his turn signal, Jennifer noticed the wooden Forest

Preserve sign. "And that's why you're going to the hayride today." He swung past the open gates and slowed. When he located Jennifer's class, he parked under a willow tree where they wouldn't be noticed.

Across the field, restless horses pawed the ground near the waiting hay rack. Nearby, Nora was huddled with Steve and Joan beside a metal grill. Lucy and Tracy were talking to a couple of boys. In another part of the field, Amy was organizing races, and Tommy and Mitch were playing touch football with several other boys.

Jennifer sat quietly taking in the scene. But her attention was directed inward. She had thought about this moment, talked to Nora about how devastated she would feel if someone she cared about ever called it quits. And now, it was here — happening! And she didn't know how she felt. She loved Tony — there was no doubt about that; she would probably always love him — and she would miss the excitement of thinking he loved her. At the same time, seeing her friends like this made her realize how much she ached to be with them.

Jason appeared suddenly in the distance. He dropped his skateboard on the narrow cement walk and jumped on, all in one smooth motion. Jennifer laughed.

Following her gaze, Tony said, "That's some maneuver!"

"Bomb drop," Jennifer said.

"He's really good at it," Tony said, admiration in his voice.

"Jason's full of surprises," Jennifer said.

"So are you, Jen," Tony said. "That's why I hope we can go on . . . becoming friends?"

Jennifer cocked her head to look at him. "Aren't we friends now?"

"It's a process," Tony said. "One that never ends."

Jennifer smiled. She could see through the fog of sadness to a sunny place. "You mean we'll always be friends?"

Tony's smile turned up the corners of his mouth and spilled into his eyes. "I sure hope so."

What a wonderful thought! No matter what else was in their lives, they could always count on one another to be there, too. "Can we shake on that?"

He took her outstretched hand and pulled her close. "We can do better than that." He kissed her.

It was quick, but it was solid. A real kiss. One she would never forget.

Without another word, she floated out of the car, picking up her pace as she approached her classmates. "Nora!" she called out.

Nora looked up, grabbed something off a nearby table, and ran toward her.

They collided in a laughing embrace, and Jennifer said, "I brought your scarf."

"Wear it," Nora said, "It looks good." She hugged Jennifer again, saying, "I knew you'd change your mind! That's why I brought this!"

"My T-shirt!" Jennifer exclaimed. She held it up. Reading, "SO MUCH TO DO . . . SO LITTLE TIME," aloud, she thought, Sometimes even a little time is enough. It can change your life. As she pulled the T-shirt on, she noticed Tony's car was still there under the willow tree. She waved.

"Jen?" Nora asked. "Are you okay?"

Jennifer turned to her. How lucky she was to have such a good friend! "More than okay," she said, repeating Tony's earlier assessment of her. "After all, a person can't sit around feeling sorry for herself." She smiled. "Life goes on."

Nora was solemn. "That's easy to say."

Jennifer giggled. "You should know. You said it first!"

Laughing, the two of them ran off to join the others.

How could Nora and Jen guess that Jason's wild stories would get them in so much trouble? Read Junior High #6, EIGHTH-GRADE HERO?